VICTORY OF THE DEAD

ANTHONY GIANGREGORIO

NOW AVAILABLE AND COMING SOON FROM UNDEAD PRESS

ZOMBIE TALES
DEADLY HUNT
CAVALCADE OF TERROR
ZOMBIE KILL: PREDATOR OR PREY?
THE NIGHT THE WORLD DIED: A ZOMBIE STORY

VICTORY OF THE DEAD

ANTHONY GIANGREGORIO

Prologue

Frank Miller of Stoneham, Massachusetts, never saw the truck that jumped the median on I-95 and hit his car head on. It happened so fast that he never felt when his body went crashing through the windshield, nor did he feel it when he landed thirty feet from his car and rolled across the road, the asphalt grinding into his flesh like a cheese grater.

He never felt the breaking of ribs, the puncture of his spleen, his stomach going up into his rib cage, nor his left arm breaking in three places.

So when all was said and done, Frank Miller never felt his death. It simply *happened*.

Paramedics arrived later to try and resuscitate him but it didn't take long for the two caregivers to realize that Frank was too far gone. They packed him up on a stretcher and slid his corpse into the back of the ambulance, then off to the hospital they went, where Frank would be pronounced dead on arrival and sent to the morgue, where he would be shoved into a cold walk-in refrigerator until time of transport.

The ambulance didn't have its flashing lights on, for there was no rush, and once they were back in Boston, the two paramedics were planning on stopping for coffee, before dumping the stiff at the hospital.

Transporting dead bodies from accident sites was a common occurrence to them, and this one should have been no different.

But something was happening in the world today, something unexplainable.

For some reason only known to God or perhaps the Devil in Hell, the dead were returning to life…and they were hungry for living flesh.

The straps on Frank Miller's body were loose, as neither paramedic was worried about the body falling off the stretcher and getting hurt. Slowly, Frank sat up, the sheet covering his upper torso falling to his lap as he slid his arms free of his bonds. His eyes were milky white, his face already pale, the lack of color to the irises happening quickly as his blood settled in his body.

In the front of the ambulance, the two men were chatting about baseball and getting laid.

Frank slid off the stretcher, the sheet falling to the floor. Frank almost fell too but he managed to stay upright. His head swiveled to face the front of the vehicle and the two men that were oblivious of their charge awakening.

With a low moan, Frank went forward and upon reaching the two men, he lunged for the driver first, sinking his teeth into the man's neck. The driver screamed as his throat was torn out and blood shot out of the wound to splash on the windshield, dashboard and on the other paramedic, who was also doing a good job at screaming.

Still chewing on the skin and muscle in his mouth, blood dripping down his chin to splash his shirt, Frank swiveled his head like an owl's and began attacking the other paramedic. The two battled for a few seconds, but the ambulance was out of control as the driver grew faint from blood loss. He was bleeding out quickly and even his own skill as a healer did little to assuage his suffering.

The ambulance swerved in its lane and crashed into another car as horns and squealing tires filled the highway. Then the ambulance jackknifed and flipped onto its side, sliding across the asphalt, sparks erupting around it. When it came to a stop, the entire highway was a massive traffic jam, more than twenty cars having become caught in the pile-up that the ambulance created.

As the ambulance tires still spun fitfully, people jumped out of their cars and ran for the vehicle, wanting to help the people that usually were there to help them.

Others called out for help, their vehicles wrecked, themselves trapped within steel cages that could mean their deaths if no one set them free.

Three men managed to get the rear doors of the ambulance open. They probably expected to find a wounded man inside, maybe even a dead one, but they sure didn't expect to find Frank Miller, his face and chest slathered with bright red blood. Frank lunged at the three Samaritans, taking down two and knocking a third to the side. Frank's already bloody teeth became bloodier as he sank them into the first man he had under him.

The other man tried to kick him off but Frank simply turned his attentions on that man, too, taking a bite out of his right hand, right below the thumb. Rearing back his head, Frank chewed on the stringy flesh as the man began to scream. Its possible the situation could have been contained, as more men and women came to the stricken victims now bleeding, but then the paramedics climbed out of the ambulance rear doors, both having died in the crash to then reanimate. The two paramedics set upon two more Samaritans and began tearing and clawing them like wild animals. Blood began to pool on the ground from multiple donors, the scarlet puddles glistening in the sun.

More victims died, to then revive and attack more arrivals The police eventually arrived, along with three more ambulances, but it wasn't long before the rescuers had succumbed to the walking dead, also, slaughtered mercilessly to then return and join their killers.

This wasn't the only horrifying tableau that was taking place across the country.

In an operating room in Florida, a man that had suffered a severe heart attack was being operated on when things took a turn for the worse. The two doctors operating worked feverishly to save the man but in the end, the heart was just too badly damaged and the man flatlined.

As the surgical staff finally gave up, one of the doctors said, "I'm calling it. Time of death is..." He checked the clock on the wall and rattled off the time.

As the doctors began to remove their masks and the nurses began to clean up, the patient suddenly sat up and lunged for the closest nurse. She screamed when his teeth sank into her cheek and tore off a large chunk, so much that her tongue could be seen flapping around within her mouth. As the nurse fell back, shrieking even louder, one of the doctors ran at the man—the man that should be dead. If the doctor needed further proof, the fact that the man's chest cavity was still gaping wide open, and that the heart had been partially removed as the two doctors had worked feverishly to save him, would have been all the information needed for a diagnosis.

The patient grabbed another nurse running past him and pulled her to him, then sank his teeth into her neck, tearing out her throat and chewing on the bloody meat. Dark blood pooled on the floor, making people slip and slide as if they were on ice.

As the doctors ran at the undead man to stop him, they soon found themselves being bitten and eaten as well. After all, who would have thought they would have to defend themselves from an attacker that wanted to eat them alive?

As the nurse with the torn-out throat bled out, she soon revived and attacked one of the doctors, thus beginning the chain of death.

It only got worse from there.

In Ohio, an eighty-five-year-old grandfather was sleeping in his easy chair. Though age had taken its toll on his body, Grandpa was still a powerful man, with broad shoulders and muscular arms and legs. Though a sedentary lifestyle had given him a belly, his physique was still better than men half his age.

At his feet, playing quietly on the carpeted floor, were his two grandchildren that he was baby-sitting while his daughter ran a few errands and enjoyed the day without her children. Lily was seven with blonde hair and blue eyes and Billy was eight, with brown hair and brown eyes. One child took after one parent, as Grandpa's daughter was blonde and his son-in-law was a brunette.

Grandpa snored loudly and the two grandchildren thought it was funny. They were so preoccupied in there playing that they didn't notice when the snoring ceased.

Within Grandpa's chest, one of the valves in his heart finally gave out and Grandpa suffered a coronary, dying in his sleep. As his bowels let go, the kids wrinkled their noses, thinking Grandpa had soiled himself again—he'd done it before.

The kids moved a little to the side, wanting to be where the air was slightly cleaner, and they went back to playing again.

When Grandpa opened his milky white eyes, the two grandchildren didn't look up. Nor did they glance his way when Grandpa slowly rose from his chair, urine and feces dripping down both legs to pool in his slippers.

His legs were unstable, as if he was a baby walking for the first time. One inch at a time, he slid his slippered feet across the floor, while droplets of brown slid off his ankles to soak into the carpet.

The sunlight came in from his back so that he projected a shadow on the two children, who were still concentrating on their game. His mouth slack, drool sliding out of the corner of his mouth to splash onto his chest, he bent over and reached out for Lily.

Before the small girl knew what was happening, a large hand wrapped around her hair and pulled her off the floor. She screamed as her scalp burned from the weight of supporting her body, and her eyes went wide as she was spun around to gaze into Grandpa's pale eyes. She continued screaming as Grandpa pulled her close, bent her head back, and sank his dentures into her slim neck.

Blood squirted between his teeth as Lily kicked harder. Grandpa was a big man, topping six feet, and Lily looked like a rag doll in his arms as he sucked her blood and chewed on her throat.

On the floor, Billy was on his feet, punching Grandpa to let his sister go. As he did this, blood dripped onto his head, to roll down his nose and then the floor. He was yelling, too, crying also, while he punched Grandpa and ordered him to let Lily go.

Grandpa didn't feel the light punches on his legs, and he chewed on Lily until he grew tired of her, then tossed her aside. The body fell to the floor, limp, half her neck gone, her head at an odd angle due to no muscles to support it.

Billy's tears clouded his vision, and when he looked up, he saw Grandpa staring down at him, his arms reaching to grab the boy. Billy realized his danger and almost escaped but he wasn't fast enough. Grandpa wrapped his beefy hands around Billy's small biceps and lifted him up and began to feed, much the same as he did Lily.

As Billy shrieked in terror and pain, on the floor, Lily was already stirring.

Billy would join her soon enough.

In Philadelphia, in the city medical building, one of the city's medical examiners was about to begin an autopsy. The 'Y' incision had already been made and the rib cage had been cracked and separated, the torso of the corpse on the steel table reassembling an open book.

The medical examiner seemed bored as he began reaching into the cadaver to start the process of removing the organs. The man on the table had died of a gunshot wound to the heart and so cause of death was already established. But due-process meant that the body would be examined in detail, to make sure there was nothing amiss other than the gunshot.

Most of the organs had been separated but not removed from the chest cavity and the examiner was removing the spleen. As he turned to place it in a stainless steel bowl, the cadaver's eyes snapped open. When the M.E. turned back to the body, he wasn't looking at the corpse's face and so didn't notice this odd occurrence. Reaching into the chest cavity, the shattered heart was extricated. The bullet was still lodged in the left ventricle, and the examiner was already thinking of how to extract it and still leave the heart relatively intact when the cadaver suddenly sat up.

"What in the world?" the M.E. said in awe, taking a step backwards. His mouth hung slack and he stared with wide eyes at the cadaver before him.

The corpse slowly turned so its legs were hanging off the gurney and then it slid to the floor. As it became upright, the loose organs within slid out to splash onto the cold tile floor. The wet slap of meat hitting the floor affected the once-hardened stomach of the M.E., causing the man to release his stomach contents. He turned to the side and vomited his last meal onto the tiles.

As he was heaving, bile dripping from his chin, the cadaver came forward and tackled the examiner like the two were playing football. They went down in a heap of limbs, the examiner landing face first in his own vomit. But he had no time to become revolted by this mess as the cadaver sank its teeth into his right cheek, then slid its cracked lips down the bloody face and began tearing into the examiner's neck. The carotid artery was torn asunder by gnashing teeth, and in seconds, the examiner would be dead, bleeding out on the floor.

The M.E.'s screams of pain alerted others to his predicament and two men and a woman ran into the room. The woman stopped cold, horrified, but the two men ran to the cadaver and tried to pull it off the bleeding examiner. As they did this, the corpse turned and grabbed one of the new arrivals by his arm and sank its teeth into the man's wrist, severing a vein and tearing a large chunk of flesh from the limb. The man screamed and punched at the corpse to release him but the cadaver had gone in for more, the teeth clamped on the arm like a steel vice. Meanwhile, the examiner had bled out, died, and now had returned, all within the space of a minute. With glazed-over eyes, the newly risen zombie reached up, grabbed the second man, and sank his teeth into the man's thigh, tearing out bits of material from the man's pants and then the skin beneath.

The young woman of twenty-three watched, terrified as the four men—one of them naked with a gaping 'Y' incision in his chest—all rolled around on the floor, resembling some giant blob with eight arms and legs. It wasn't long before the two new arrivals had suffered enough wounds that they expired, only to return moments later.

When the cadaver with the gaping hole in its chest swiveled its head to lock gazes with the woman, she began screaming, which got the attention of the other three zombies.

The group of undead extricated themselves, and as two went around one side of the table, the other two went to the right to reach the petrified woman. She was rooted to the spot. She knew all three of these men, and had dated two of them over the course of the past two years of being in the building. Only the original cadaver was unknown to her. Shaking her head in fear, she never raised a finger to defend herself as the four zombies surrounded her and took her down, tearing into her soft body, feeding on her warm flesh. She did scream a few times but then her jugular was ripped out by a set of teeth and her suffering was mercilessly cut short.

In time, the zombies stepped away from her as she rose from death, and the five animated corpses left the room and moved deeper into the building.

More screams filled the corridors soon enough, as well as gunshots, but no one understood what was happening and so didn't know how to deal with the situation.

For how do you stop Death itself when it comes for you?

Chapter 1

Bunker Hill University. One mile outside of Boston, Mass.

"Okay, class, our time's about up for this week so until we meet again, I want you to read chapter four through eight in your text books," Professor Allen said.

"Hey, Shane, over here," Greg said in a loud whisper, wanting to get his friend's attention.

A pencil flew across the room, heading for Shane Garrett's head. Before it could hit Shane, Prof. Allen stepped into the path, and was hit right between the eyes, his glasses then knocked from his face to fall onto the floor. Picking them up, he checked to see that they were intact before placing them back on his rather large nose.

He glared at Greg, the boy who'd thrown the pencil, then at Shane. "I'll see you both after class please."

"Me? What did I do?" Shane asked but Prof. Allen only glared at him further.

The class went on for another thirty minutes and then Prof. Allen dismissed everyone. Shane stayed in his seat while Greg tried to sneak out the door.

"And where do you think you're going?" Prof. Allen asked Greg.

Greg dove for the nearest chair, spilling the papers that were in his folder onto the floor. He looked at the papers, shrugged, and sighed. "I didn't want to miss the next train on the Orange line, sir."

"I'm not going to bother chastising you, Greg, but you already have a low test score and it doesn't look like you're going to pass my class if you don't apply yourself more. You paid for this class, at least you could do is pass it. Now, out."

Greg ran out, waving goodbye to Shane. Prof. Allen cleared his throat before addressing Shane directly. "And Shane, your test scores aren't much better. Have you considered getting a tutor?"

Shane put on a straight face. "No, not really"

"Well, you should."

Shane shrugged. "Prof. Allen, I only came to this community college because I promised my dad before he left to fight in Iraq that I would. See, with me in college, I'm the first Garret male to ever do so. I wanted to make him proud but now that he's dead I don't see why I should stay anymore. It's a waste of…" He trailed off.

Prof. Allen sat on the edge of his desk, rubbing the bridge of his nose where his eyeglasses had left a mark. "I know about your father dying in the war over there and let me tell you I'm so sorry for your loss. Look, Shane, you show true signs of potential. Your test scores are good when you want to apply yourself. But you seem to lack the inner motivation to want to do better. Way is that?"

"I don't know."

"Sure you do, Shane, you just have to look deep within yourself and really take a good look at who you are, who you want to be."

"Prof. Allen, I do my best in this class, all right? Maybe I like playing video games more than college, as if that's such a shock. My dad's dead, all right? He's why I'm here. He's gone now but I'm still here. Now it's just me and my mom and she's not taking it much better than I am." He stood up. "I'm leaving now, Professor, thank you for your concern."

Prof. Allen sighed heavily, tired of the same old thing. He tried to motivate these young adults and they ignored everything he said. Waving his hand in defeat, he simply said, "Well, I just want you to know that I'm here for you if you need me. Go 'head and get going, you don't want to miss your train."

Shane gathered his book bag and left, his footsteps echoing down the hall. He crossed the quad and walked down the pathway that led to the Orange line for the Boston subway system. The 'T' as it was called locally.

The platform was empty so he took a seat on one of the benches and pulled out his Ipod. Jamming the earbuds into his ears, he cranked up some AC/DC, closed his eyes, and tried not to think about what Prof. Allen had said.

The professor had unknowingly stirred up all the loss and grief Shane felt for his father once more. His dad had been a decorated war hero and when Shane was younger, he'd considered him to be more of a superhero than a man. Shane had been eighteen when his father left the last time, he and his mother not knowing that the man would never return from this tour in Iraq, that an IED would kill him and his team on a lonely stretch of deserted highway in the middle of nowhere.

Before his father had left on that fateful last tour, Shane had been sitting on the back porch of his house, listening to music as he often did. It had been a cool summer night and his father had come out and joined him, then he'd handed Shane a beer, which had surprised Shane a lot. His father had a beer of his own, too.

"Hey, son," his father had said upon sitting down next to Shane on the steps. "Can we talk?"

Shane had pulled off his headphones. "Sure, Dad, what's up?"

"I'm leaving in the morning, you know that." It was a statement, not a question.

Shane nodded.

"Before I left, I thought we should talk, you know, just father and son."

"What about?"

"About you, son, and the man you're growing up to be. Look, I watch you sometimes when you don't think I am and I see how you are. How you act with your friends, how you look at life. Your moral code, if you will."

"Yeah?" Shane took a sip of the cold beer.

"Well, sometimes I worry about you, about who you might be. If something happens to me, I still want be there in some way to steer you in the right direction. So I want you to start doing something for me."

"Yeah?"

"Whenever you're in a situation where you need to man up, I want you to imagine me standing behind you, and whatever you choose to do in that situation, I want you to think if I would approve. Can you do that for me?"

"Geez, Dad, I don't know, I mean…"

"No, you don't have to say anything else. But listen, after I'm gone tomorrow, just think about it okay? Remember, you can do what you want, make the choices you want, because I won't be there to stop you, but what if I was? Would you be proud of the decisions you were making? That's all, think about it, okay?"

"Sure, Dad, I can do that."

"Good. I love you, son, you know that, right?"

"Yeah, Dad, I love you, too."

He playfully rubbed Shane's hair. After that they hadn't talked, but simply sat together while drinking their beers. The next morning, before Shane woke up, his father was gone…forever.

Chapter 2

After the train dropped Shane off at the station near his house, where he would then take a bus the rest of the way home, he decided that he didn't want to go home yet as it was only two in the afternoon, so he went to his childhood friend, Susan's house, knowing she was home today.

Susan Griffin was a beautiful, smart, kind, sexy girl. Shane had known her since elementary school. Unfortunately she had a boyfriend. His name was Dean Jenkins and though Shane tried not to like him out of jealousy, he had to admit that the guy was all right.

Shane arrived at Susan's house a little before three, knocked once, then entered like he always did. Susan's parents both worked late on weekdays, so she had the house to herself until dinner. Unlike Shane, she hadn't chosen to go to college and instead had gotten a job as an intern at an office building in Boston.

She was an only child like Shane which was one of the reasons they had stayed friends over the years.

As Shane entered the living room, announcing himself as he did, he found Dean and Susan sitting on the leather sofa, wrapped in each other's arms. They were making out. Jealousy burned inside Shane, but instead of showing how upset he was, he dropped down into the matching plush chair that went with the couch and crossed his arms on his chest. Eventually, Susan and Dean came up for air and noticed him.

"Hey, Shane, good to see ya. How long've you been there?" Dean asked.

Shane shrugged nonchalantly. "Long enough. You two should just do it and get it over with already." He wanted to say more but held his tongue. He knew Susan wasn't sleeping with Dean, as she wanted to save herself for marriage. She'd been embarrassed when she'd told Shane this, but deep down he'd loved her even more upon hearing it. That meant he still had a chance with her.

After an awkward silence, Susan asked, "Anything new going on?"

"Nah, same old shit, I guess," Shane said. "My professor gave me some crap today. I know the guy is just looking out for me but it gets old after a while, ya know?" He paused. "He even brought up my dad."

"Really? Wow, he was trying to pull on your heartstrings, huh?" Susan said as she got up from the couch. "You want something to drink?"

"Sure, why not, a coke would be great," Shane said, Dean agreeing also by holding his hand up and showing two fingers.

Dean stared at Shane and vice versa for a few seconds until Susan returned with the drinks, handing one to each of them. "So, what do we do now?"

Dean glared at Shane, his eyes saying that Shane was the third wheel but Shane ignored the look and smiled. "How 'bout a movie from your horror collection?"

"That's a great idea," she said excitedly. "Isn't it, Dean?"

He forced a smile. "Sure, yeah. Great."

She padded off to her bedroom to retrieve a movie while Dean glared at Shane even harder. Shane merely smiled back and sipped his drink.

"Here we go, here's a good one. It's a new zombie flick I just got the other day."

"Zombies?" Dean said. "Oh, man, I hate zombies. It's all so fake."

"Well, I like them, Susan," Shane said to her.

"Oh, what a shock," Dean muttered.

A few minutes later, the television was on, and as Susan went to the DVD player and popped the disc in, the news was on, talking about some situation on Interstate 95. Before more could be heard, Susan pressed the input button on the TV so that the television would receive the DVD signal, then she hit play and got comfortable on the couch beside Dean.

"Oh man, I can't wait to see this," she said and curled up close to Dean, who grinned slyly at Shane as he wrapped his arm around Susan.

Shane said nothing, pretending he was concentrating on the movie, but the entire time, out of the corner of his eye, he had his eye on Susan, wishing it was he that she was curling up next to.

Chapter 3

A few hours later, Shane left Susan's house and began to walk home. Night had fallen and it was dark. There was a shortcut behind Susan's house that shaved ten minutes off his walk so he decided to go that way. He'd taken this way so many times that he barely paid attention to where he was going. Upon leaving the house, he'd seen that his mother had left him three messages on his cell phone but he ignored them.

He would be home soon enough and for now, he felt like being alone with his thoughts and sometimes his mother had a way of bringing up the past a little too much. She had loved her husband dearly and when the grief was too much, she sought consolation with Shane, who was still dealing with his own loss.

The path took him past an old, rusty playground, no longer in use. When he and Susan were kids, they used to come here all the time and play. Back then, the laughter of children was a common occurrence, the playground a popular destination for mothers to bring their children and relax on the surrounding benches and gab with other moms.

No one went there now, though, not even the teenagers to drink on Friday and Saturday nights. A few years ago, a brutal killing had happened there and since then there was a rumor it was haunted. Just a story but still, when it was dark and silent, it was still creepy as hell. There were street lamps surrounding the area, but all the bulbs were either burned out or broken, the city not bothering to fix them. The swings were all but rusted away and hung motionless, the paint on the see-saw peeling and flaking to expose the rust beneath.

Strolling past the playground, the wind must have pushed a swing, because Shane heard the unearthly sound of rusty metal scraping against rusty metal. He stopped walking and stared at the dark playground, but there was nothing there. Curious, he went closer, despite an inner voice telling him that he was crazy. In every horror movie he'd ever seen, when the person in the movie heard a sound, they went to investigate, instead of getting the hell out of there. And now here he was doing the same thing like an idiot. Besides, he had zombies on the brain from the movie he'd watched at Susan's house and he felt that this made him extra nervous.

Suddenly, out of the overgrown bushes near the swings, something moved. There was a rustle of branches and Shane flinched, dropping his backpack and reaching into his pocket for anything to fight back with. There was nothing. Searching the ground around him, he picked up a fallen branch about the thickness of his wrist. Holding it like a club, he felt a little better.

But despite knowing how foolish he was being, ever so cautiously, he went to the bushes, trying to see inside them. He was beginning to think maybe it was just a skunk or raccoon, when a hand shot out between the branches and grabbed his arm—hard.

Shane jerked back, raising the club, and was about to bring it down on what he believed was an attacker, when the clouds shifted overhead and allowed the moonlight to filter through, bathing the park in pallid light. Shane saw it was an old friend he used to hang out with back in high school. His name was Tim Shannon. He hadn't seen Tim in years, and he'd thought Tim had gone off to college himself, New Hampshire University if he was right. But here was Tim now...not looking so good.

Blood covered Tim's body from head to toe, his pupils faded to a pale white. He was bleeding from a large gash in his throat, the blood seeping out of the wound and onto his clothes.

Shane dropped the branch and went to Tim. "Jesus, Tim, is that you? What the fuck happened to you! Are you all right?" The second he asked the last question he realized how stupid it sounded. Of course Tim wasn't all right. He looked like he'd been attacked by a wolf or a rabid dog. You didn't hear about stuff like that happening much anymore but every now and then a pit bull got out of its yard or a wolf came down from the nearby hills.

Tim opened his mouth to speak, but instead emitted a distressed groan. Shane withdrew his cell phone and dialed 9-1-1. "I'm calling for help," he said. When an operator answered, he practically screamed into the phone, "Hello? My name's Shane Garrett. I need help. I found my friend in the old park off of Bayside. I think he's dying!"

Chapter 4

Susan and Dean met Shane at the Emergency Room lobby after he called them, and his own mother. Shane sat in a corner of the waiting room, staring at the wall, his face drawn as he thought back to when he'd found his friend in the park.

Tim had fallen unconscious soon after Shane had called for help and seven minutes after the call, an ambulance arrived. The paramedics were stumped as to what had caused his injuries. They put an oxygen mask on his mouth and placed him on a stretcher, then wheeled him to the back of the ambulance. They let Shane come too, as he was the one who'd called them.

Across the Emergency Room lobby, near the doors leading into the main wing, stood Tim's parents and sister, as well as Shane's mother. They all wore faces of concern and Tim's mother had been crying. Shane had talked to them for a few minutes and then left them alone.

"How is he?" Susan asked and sat down next to Shane. Dean took a chair on the other side.

Shane shook his head. "Last time I heard the nurse update Tim's parents they said he was still unconscious."

"What the fuck happened to him?" Dean asked.

"How the hell should I know? I was cutting through the woods, past the old playground, and he was there looking like he'd been attacked by some wild animal. It was awful."

"Shit, that's terrible," Dean said, looking right at Shane. "I use the path past the playground all the time. It could have been me that was attacked or even Susan."

Susan stood up and went to Tim's parents, talking to them for a few moments. She hugged Tim's mother, then returned to Shane and Dean. "They don't know much more than what you just said," she informed Shane. "Last they heard, he was in critical condition and the doctors won't let them see him."

They sat in silence for a while, watching people move back and forth. At one time Susan left to make a call on her cell phone to inform her own parents what was going on. When she returned she said, "I was listening to some nurses talking why they were on a smoke break and it seems Tim isn't the only one who's been attacked. The Emergency Room is filling up with case after case."

"Jesus, what the hell is going on?" Dean whispered.

Before anyone could reply, a bloody man came stumbling into the lobby with the help of two other people. "We need help here!" one of the people carrying the bloody man yelled.

"What happened?" a nurse said as she ran up to them.

"We were leaving a bar down on Maple Street and this guy came out of nowhere and attacked Matt. The guy fucking bit him!"

"Follow me, we'll get you right in," the nurse said. "Do you have insurance?" She asked, her voice fading as they left the lobby and moved deeper into the Emergency Room, past the double sliding doors that led into the section with beds. The wounded man was moaning the entire time.

When the tableau was over, another nurse entered the lobby through the sliding doors, her eyes searching for someone. When she saw Tim's parents, she began walking to them. Shane saw this, stood up, and left the waiting room and entered the lobby, cutting her off.

"How's Tim?" he asked. "He's an old friend. I'm the one who found him."

Susan and Dean joined Shane, standing directly behind him. The nurse's gaze swept over each of them, and after a few moments, she muttered something that rocked Shane hard.

"I'm not supposed to tell you, as you're not immediate family," the nurse said. "But I can tell you all care for your friend. He's…I'm afraid he's dead. I need to tell his parents, so if you'll excuse me. I'm so sorry for your loss." The look in the nurse's eyes told Shane how bad she felt. Susan collapsed into a chair, tears springing from her eyes, her mascara running down her cheeks. Dean sat next to her, wrapping his arm around her and hugging her. Shane watched as the nurse told Tim's parents of his death and Shane saw his own mother lower her head in sadness. Though Tim was dead, no one wanted to leave, at least not yet, and everyone stayed in the lobby, each focused on their own inner loss.

Finally, Susan said, "It's late, Shane. I should go, my parents are gonna be worried." She rubbed her eyes.

"Yeah, okay."

Dean stood up too and led Susan away, and with a slight wave, they left, leaving Shane alone. Across the lobby in the waiting room, Shane's mother was sitting alone after Tim's parents had been allowed to see the body of their son.

He got up, crossed the lobby, and entered the waiting room, joining her. "I think there's nothing more we can do here, Mom We should go," he said in a low voice.

"Oh, honey, I'm so sorry for Tim. I know you two used to be close."

"Yeah, well, that was years ago back in high school." He glanced down at his clothes, as if seeing the blood for the first time—Tim's blood. He suddenly wanted a shower more than anything else in the world.

She slowly stood up and hugged him and he accepted it, then they walked side by side to the elevator to leave.

Just as the elevator doors closed and began to go down to the main floor, one of the Emergency room nurses began to scream, and then Tim's parents joined in, and soon after that, more followed.

Chapter 5

As civil unrest grew worse, the National Guard was called in the next day, though it was done quietly, so as not to cause more panic. A helicopter leaving Hanscom Air Force base was supposed to go to Rhode Island, but unfortunately, the helicopter developed catastrophic engine trouble not long after taking off, and the pilot was forced to make an emergency landing in a rural area outside of Boston, which didn't go as planned.

Including the pilot, there had been eight men in the chopper. Corporal Brett Johnson was one of them.

He was the only one to drag his battered but intact body out of the wreckage. He had cuts on his legs and upper torso, and his left wrist hurt, but when he tried to move it, he found he could, though it pained him to do so. He was lightheaded from shock, and he'd lost some blood. He felt no self pity for his plight, however, after seeing the other men in the helicopter. He knew he was lucky to be alive.

He limped over to the cockpit and peered inside. The pilot had a piece of steel sticking out from between his helmet, his visor cracked.

His eyes, which were barely visible, were open and vacant in death, and Johnson didn't have to check for a pulse to know that the man was dead.

A piece of the ruined rotors protruded from the ground at a bent angle fifty feet away, and more wreckage was scattered across the crash site.

A few severed limbs could be seen as well and Johnson looked away, his stomach churning as bile crept into his throat.

Going to the rear of the downed aircraft, he found more bodies relatively intact amidst a charnel house of body parts. He spotted the first aid kit and went to it, then went back outside to cautiously clean and bandage his wounds.

The cuts weren't as bad as he first thought, the blood making it look worse than it was. He wrapped his bad wrist up with an Ace bandage, wincing with the pain as he did it one-handed. Then he swallowed some Motrin to ease the pain. He went back into the helicopter to see if there was anything else he could use.

One of the bodies was missing its head, and he assumed it was somewhere around in the wreckage.

Blood flowed down the body from the diagonal cut in the neck that had taken the head clean off, and sharp debris poked out of the corpse wherever Johnson looked. Another body was crushed between two gun crates.

Another of the bodies was in an even worse state. Its arms and legs were gone, and the corpse's skull was cracked nearly down the middle; pinkish-red brain matter seeped through the crack.

He began to taste bile again and he had to look away and close his eyes.

When his stomach settled slightly, he went through the bodies and any supplies he could find, taking with him some bottled water, some dry food and a few other odds and ends he thought might come in handy, including an M-16A with two extra clips.

Needless to say, Johnson knew he was one of the luckiest men in the world to have survived this crash with only minor wounds.

Not knowing if the pilot managed to get off a mayday before going down, Johnson knew he needed to contact Hanscom and report what had happened.

His cell phone was in his pocket, but when he pulled it out, it fell apart in his hand, destroyed in the crash. He searched the other bodies, but either there were no phones to be found or the ones he did were also inoperable. So much for technology, he thought.

He examined his surroundings.

He could sum it all up in three words—middle of nowhere.

Austere land surrounded him on all sides, and off in the distance, he could see what looked like a farm.

There were rolling fields of grass. He slung the rifle over his shoulder, and began walking to the farm.

Chapter 6

With a heavy limp, Johnson crossed the land until reaching the farm house. It wasn't anything special. The roof had been patched in a few places with roofing tar and the paint on the house itself was peeling. A three foot fence surrounded the home and the grass needed to be cut. A few lawn gnomes peered out between some of the tall blades, as if watching the new arrival with interest.

Johnson suddenly felt cold and began to sweat. He assumed it was from his wounds, his body in shock. He felt terrible and though he didn't want any, he forced himself to drink some water, knowing he needed to regain his strength.

The scent of grass was in the air and the odor made him feel sicker. Damn allergies, he figured. It made him want to sneeze, but if started, he knew he wouldn't be able to stop.

He walked up to the house and knocked on the front door. It creaked, and slowly opened to a dark, empty house. He heard a sound and took a step backwards, the rifle ready. He didn't give it much thought that it was he who was the intruder here; all he could think about was contacting Hanscom.

The sound came again and he realized it was just an errant breeze that had shaken a tree branch, to brush against the corner of the house. Johnson let out a small nervous laugh, feeling silly for being so jumpy.

"Hello, is anyone home? Hello? In case you didn't hear it, there was an accident on your land, a chopper crashed." There was no reply.

Taking a step inside the house, he began checking the rooms.

The house seemed normal enough. There was a large oak dining room table with four wooden chairs around it, a set of stairs going up to the second floor, and a fireplace surrounded by a comfortable looking sofa and rocking chair, as well as a television set that looked like it was thirty years old, right down to the rabbit ears on the top. Johnson turned on the television and was greeted with static. He turned it off.

He walked in the direction of the stairs leading to the second floor. Going to the landing, he wrapped his left hand around the handrail, then winced when his sore wrist flared up.

He walked up the stairs cautiously, the shadows seeming to jump out at him and grab him. There were pictures on the wall, showing a loving older couple and two kids. Johnson couldn't be sure but the photo looked like grandparents with their grandkids.

There were three bedrooms in the small hallway: a boy's room and a girl's room and probably the grandparents' room. He could tell two of the rooms belonged to children because each door had a small sign with a name on it. Entering the girl's room first, he saw that the room had wallpaper with unicorns on it, and statues of unicorns were all over the place. The girl obviously was a unicorn fan. The boy's room was painted red with baseball posters on the walls. Baseball cards were on the dresser and a worn baseball glove sat beside them. Both rooms had a layer of dust on the surfaces, telling him that his initial thought was correct. The rooms were for the grandkids when they came to stay at the house.

"Empty." He told himself, more to hear his voice and break the silence. He checked the grandparents' room as well, finding it also empty, then went back down to the first floor and entered the kitchen. There were stairs here, also, leading down to the basement.

A thump from the basement broke the silence.

Cold sweat ran down his forehead, and Johnson felt a headache growing deep in his head, right between his eyes. His imagination went wild on what might be down in that cellar. He snatched a long, sharp knife from a cutting block on the counter, knowing the rifle wasn't good for in-close fighting. Then he approached the steps with his rifle slung over his shoulder.

One step at a time, he walked down the creaking, wooden stairs into the darkness. He used the hand with the knife to feel along the wall for a light switch, but was unable to find one. The panic grew inside him, causing him to nearly scream out in fear. An inner voice told him to turn around, that he was being an idiot for coming down here. What did he hope to find?

Finally reaching the bottom step and then the floor, he crouched in the Stygian darkness, letting his eyes focus a little before he walked anywhere. As his eyes grew accustomed to the dark, he realized it wasn't as dark as he first thought, thanks to the light coming in from the open door at the top of the stairs. He heard something shuffle across the basement at the far end, and he followed it with his ears but not his eyes.

Suddenly, light flooded the basement and Johnson was blinded for a few seconds. Someone had turned on the overhead lights. He squeezed his eyes closed out of instinct and knew he was as vulnerable as a person could be in this type of a situation.

The footsteps sounded again, this time from his right, then before he could act, someone came at him, mumbling something about, "Get the hell out of my house."

Johnson frantically thrashed out, fighting back, dropping the knife as he reached up to pull the hands away from his neck. The grip on him was powerful, and Johnson fought the growing panic within him.

"Let me go! Get off me!" he yelled out in fury. There had to be something he could do! He was a soldier after all.

Remembering his training, he recalled a move he'd learned in boot camp. He grabbed the arm of the attacker, bent at the hip, and sent the attacker flying over his head, the attacker crying out on pain and fear as he went sailing through the air. Johnson had dropped the knife to do this but it was worth it to free himself.

Then, acting swiftly, Johnson bent over and picked up the knife, rallied his courage, and ran at the person with the knife leading the way. He stabbed the attacker several times, each time making him feel more confident. Warm blood coated him, but he didn't care. He kept going to the point where he didn't know if he could stop. Finally, he paused and stepped away from the fallen form. He checked for a pulse but found none, and saw it was a man. A man Johnson had killed. He'd never taken a life before and he found it horrifying and exhilarating all at the same time. He examined the person further.

The man looked around seventy years old or so, with a beer belly. He wore faded and patched overalls, and looked like a typical farmer. His balding head had patches of white hair on it, and he had a white beard that was in need of a trim. Johnson didn't think about how he'd just committed murder and a home invasion, that he'd come into this man's house, and when attacked, had killed him. The farmer had only been defending himself and his home, and Johnson had murdered him for it. Something to think about, but not at this particular moment.

He cleaned the knife on the dead man's shirt, then unslung his rifle from his shoulder. He took a look around the room now that he could see. Approaching a metal cabinet, he opened it to see it full of cans of paint, jars of nails and screws, and paint brushes. Searching some more, he found more odds and ends associated with a handyman's workshop.

There was a workbench across the room and on the wall was a peg board with hanging tools of all types. Everything was neat and clean and Johnson nodded in approval. The farmer had been well organized. Suddenly, a wave of nausea overtook him and he closed his eyes and leaned against the cabinet. The adrenaline was fading and he felt weak and tired. His bad wrist was throbbing too from the exertion he'd put on it.

There was a wooden stool by the workbench and he sat down on it, closing his eyes as his head pounded with pain. That inner voice wanted to discus how he'd just killed a man in cold blood but he forced it down, not wanting to think about it. But the voice told him how he would be in very big trouble, how when crime scene techs arrived to investigate, they would find his DNA and fingerprints all over the place. He would be court-martialed, sent to prison for the rest of his life.

He needed to cover his tracks. But how?

Before he could consider this further, he heard the sound of shuffling feet behind him, followed by a low moan. Instinctively, he spun around. The lights went out again and he looked up at the naked bulbs—or where they were as it was now dark—not understanding what was going on. Wary, he backed up into the nearest corner and stood his ground, trying to adjust his eyes to the darkness he now found himself in.

Then a figure came out of the shadows and tried to grab him. Johnson felt adrenaline viciously pump into his veins again, and he lashed out, pushing the attacker away and shooting the M-16 into the darkness. If he hit something or someone, he didn't hear any sounds of pain.

A low moaning came then and the lights suddenly turned back on, blinding Johnson once again, and he realized there wasn't someone flicking a switch but that the entire power grid was fluctuating.

The farmer was on his feet somehow, the stab wounds still evident on his body, blood pooling on the floor from the fresh bullet holes he'd just received.

Johnson wasn't putting two and two together, that the dead were returning to life. All he saw was that a man he'd just killed was now up and walking again.

The old man moaned once more. Blood filled the farmer's mouth and when he opened it, the dark fluid dribbled out to splatter onto the floor.

When the old man charged him, Johnson leveled the rifle and fired, riddling the old man's chest with half a dozen rounds, but the farmer didn't stop. When the old man reached him, Johnson used the butt of the M-16 and hit the man's chin with it, then he turned the rifle to the side and swung the weapon like a club. The farmer crumpled, his face striking the cement floor hard. Looking down, Johnson saw teeth now mixed with the blood under the old man's face.

Johnson mumbled a silent prayer and pulled the trigger on the rifle, sending a single round into the man's head. The bullet took off half the farmer's face, the lower jaw sliding three feet across the floor. The limbs spasmed as nerve endings shut down for good.

Johnson went to the stool and slumped onto it, feeling as if he was going to vomit. At first he thought he had it under control, but then his stomach heaved and the water he'd consumed, as well as small bits from his past meal, erupted out of his mouth, burning his throat in its passage.

He closed his eyes and tried to calm himself, doing his best to ignore the odor of cordite, blood and feces, as the farmer had shit himself previously upon his death.

No one had ever told him this would be the kind of day he'd have when he joined the National Guard. Hell, he was only supposed to be messing around on the weekends once a month, not murdering people in their homes.

When he was confident he could walk without falling down, he stood up and went back upstairs, taking the steps slowly and cautiously.

He looted the kitchen, taking canned goods and bottles of juice. Though the power was intermittent, the refrigerator was still relatively cold and he took out a bottle of milk and a leftover roast, as well as a bowl of salad, then ate what he could, despite not having much of an appetite. His sore wrist was a mass of burning muscle and he went to the bathroom and opened the medicine chest. There was a bottle of aspirin and he took four, then pocketed the small white bottle for later. He knew he would need to take more soon. He quickly washed his face and hands, then redressed his wounds with items found in the bathroom.

It was time to go.

He checked the landline in the house but the phone was dead, a telling portent of what was happening to him, he thought.

When he had everything he needed, he placed it all in a rucksack he found in a closet and then placed the sack at the front door. But he wasn't ready to leave just yet and he went to the stove and turned on the gas, then made sure all the windows were closed.

Grabbing the rucksack, he left the house, closing the door behind him. The M-16 was held tightly in his grip, his head snapping left to right, as if he expected someone to jump out at him at any moment.

He went to the side of the farmhouse to see if the old farmer had a car or a pickup truck. He found an old Ford truck in a weathered barn but it wasn't in any condition to be driven. He did discover a map in the glove box and he found the nearest hospital, knowing his wounds needed to be looked at by a trained medical team, and not his half-ass idea of doctoring.

St. Charles Hospital showed on the map, around ten miles away. So be it, he thought. Besides, he could really go for some painkillers right about now, not the shitty aspirin he was taking. He could call a cab when he was back in civilization, or if it came to it, he could commandeer a car.

He left the farm and began walking down the dusty dirt driveway, then stopped when he was fifty feet away. Turning to face the house, he lined up the rifle where the kitchen was located, and fired off a three round burst.

The bullets sliced through the thin wall of the house as if it was paper and ignited the natural gas filling the home. The house exploded in a blazing fireball that sent half the roof flying away and knocked down the walls. He watched the flames coming out of the hole in the roof for a few seconds, satisfied that the inferno was going good, then began moving away.

The fire would destroy any evidence of him killing the farmer.

He was limping and he winced every time he added pressure to his right leg. The smell of smoke came to him as he walked and he glanced over his shoulder one time before the house was out of view.

The entire structure was burning brightly, and every now and then a secondary explosion went off as the gas lines throughout the house ignited.

The Scorched Earth policy. He had to say that he liked it. And after all; were you really doing something wrong if no one knew you did it?

He laughed to himself, thinking that terribly witty.

Chapter 7

On the drive home with his mother, there had been something on the radio about incidents involving attacks and deaths but neither had been interested and Shane had turned off the radio. They were both in a melancholy mood, they didn't need to hear about the horrors of the world at the moment.

They were only a few blocks from home when his mother pulled up to a five-way intersection and stopped at the red light. This red light was always a killer and took almost a full four minutes to rotate.

A few cars drove past on the opposite side and they sat silently together. Then she slid her hand across the seat and took his, squeezing it gently. "I'm so sorry about your friend, Shane," she said, her voice sounding as if she was going to cry.

"Thanks, Mom." Then he realized she was becoming emotional and he looked her in the eyes as she returned the gaze. "What's wrong? Something tells me you're not choked up because of Tim."

She shook her head, her dark hair falling across her face. She brushed it back and sniffled. "No, I suppose not. I was thinking of your father and how you're all I have left. If that had been you in the hospital, well, I don't know want I would do if I ever lost you."

"I'm not going anywhere, Mom, you're stuck with me."

She laughed, though it seemed forced. "I see. You're getting more like your father every day." She reached out and grabbed his chin, then moved his head to study his features. "And just as handsome, I might add."

"Ah, Mom, cut it out."

Suddenly, there was a loud thump to his mother's left and they both turned to see a man slapping the window of the driver's door, his knees having connected with the door itself. He was slapping at the window as if he was deranged.

"Oh my God, what does he want?" his mother yelled as the man continued to slap the window. The glass was open a few inches at the top so some air could get into the car and the man tried to slide his fingers into the opening. His mother screamed and slid closer to Shane, who had to admit he was flabbergasted.

The man continued to slap the glass, leaving behind a trail of what sure as hell looked like blood. His face was pale, the eyes milky white, the clothes disheveled. Shane was pretty sure the man was homeless—a bum—and by the looks of it in need of medication of some kind desperately.

A low moan came from the man's throat as he licked the glass, leaving behind another trail of mucus. A horn sounded from behind them and then another as the traffic light changed from red to green.

Shane saw this too and slapped his mother on the shoulder. "The light's green, Mom! Go, get going!"

"But the man!" she cried,

"Forget him! Just go!"

She did as he said and stepped on the gas pedal, the car surging forward. The man was pushed away as the car slid out from under him and he stumbled into traffic. Others cars drove around the man, more than one honking at the idiot in the middle of the street.

His mother drove through the intersection and let out a loud sigh of relief when she knew the man was behind her. Shane turned around to see what was going on with the man and he saw the bum still wandering the street, cars and trucks having to go around him. Then the crazy man was lost from sight as the car turned another corner.

"Oh my Lord, that was terrifying," his mother said. "What was wrong with him?"

Shane shrugged. "Probably mentally unstable. I learned in history how Reagan let all the mental patients out into the world to save some cash. Maybe that guy is one of them."

"Well, I'm just glad my window was rolled up. If it hadn't been…" She trailed off but Shane knew what she meant. Things might have been much more problematic if the window hadn't been up.

"It's times like this when I really miss your father," she said and sat taller in her seat, trying to compose herself. "He would have known what to do."

Shane smiled. "Dad probably would have gotten out of the car and beat the hell out of that guy for scratching the paint."

"You're probably right, honey, but I bet after that he would have personally brought the man to the hospital. Your father was kind like that, always thinking of others."

"Huh, yeah, Mom, you're right, he probably would have done that exact thing." Images of his father went through his mind and he felt calmer, his father the rock in the storm in his head that he would hold on to.

They pulled into the driveway and his mother turned off the engine and let out a deep breath. "There, we made it in one piece, despite crazy people and everything else in this world." She grabbed her purse from the seat and opened her door. "Are you hungry, Shane? Despite everything that's happened today I'm starving. I haven't eaten since breakfast."

Shane wasn't very hungry but he could tell by the way his mother was looking at him that she needed the company.

"Sure, Mom, I can eat."

She leaned over and kissed his cheek, then rubbed it to wipe away the lipstick she'd left there. "Good, dinner's on in twenty."

Chapter 8

That night, Shane lay in his bed, staring up at the ceiling, thinking about the horrible day he'd had. He could hear his mother messing around in the kitchen, no doubt clearing what was left of the dinner table. He'd told her he would help but she'd simply rushed him off.

He had homework for college to do but he didn't want to do it, knowing his mind would never be able to focus.

Outside, a siren screamed down the street, and then another. That was odd. His neighborhood was usually very quiet. As he lay there, his thoughts went to Susan. He wished he was with her now. He closed his eyes and imagined him walking into her house, the lights on low, a few candles set up in the living room. She would invite him to sit down on the couch. He would ask about Dean and she would tell him that it was over between them and that she'd finally realized that Shane was the one she wanted.

She would stand before him as he sat on the couch and slowly undress, until she was wearing nothing but her bra and panties. The candlelight would caress her body and then she would sit on his lap and take his hands, placing them on each breast.

"I want you, Shane. Make love to me. I need to feel you inside me," she'd breathe.

Reaching back, she would take off her bra and push his face into her cleavage. Then in time, he would undress and the two of them would make passionate love on the carpeted floor, then on the couch and the easy chair.

Finally, both of them spent and lying side by side on the floor by the couch, she would roll over to look at him, her hair cascading over her face and say, "I love you, Shane. I always have "

The alarm clock began to shriek its persuasive wail and Shane's eyes snapped open. He had to take a quick look around the room, and slowly it dawned on him that he was in his bed, and had been since last night. He'd drifted off to sleep and had ended up having one hell of a dream.

As he sat up in bed, he felt sticky down below and to his embarrassment he found he'd had an orgasm in his sleep. This brought images of the dream to the forefront of his mind and visions of Susan came to him. He shook his groggy head clear and got up, then bundled his bedclothes into a ball and tossed it all into the hamper, including his clothes he'd still been wearing upon falling asleep. Shit, what was he, twelve? To have an orgasm while he was sleeping?

Rubbing his face to wake up, he went to the bathroom to shower, use the toilet, and get his day going.

He had three classes at Bunker Hill today.

Chapter 9

There was something going on at the platform for the 'T'. A crowd had gathered and from what Shane could see, it looked like some homeless guy was going crazy and trying to attack anyone that got too close. But when the crowd shifted slightly, Shane got a better look at the man, and saw that the apparent homeless man was wearing a three piece suit and expensive leather shoes. Then the man was lost from sight as the Transit Police arrived and arrested him.

Shane would have kept watching but his train arrived and he didn't want to be late for class. The train was full as it was every morning, rush hour being in full swing. The only advantage was that by the time he reached his stop, the train was usually half-empty.

The passengers all had that same glazed-over look of commuters, like zombies that had become domesticated, their eyes vacant of emotion. No one looked at anyone, as if it was some kind of taboo to make eye contact with another human being. Most were staring at cell phones, Kindles or ipads, a few even reading real paperbacks.

Shane acted the same, and when he was able to get a seat, he propped open one of his text books to try to get in some studying.

A few people were talking, always in hushed voices, and with the clatter of the wheels on the tracks, it was hard to hear what they were saying, but Shane could have sworn he heard words like: attacked, guy took three bullets, some kind of infection. Then the words were lost in the cacophony of the train.

When his stop arrived, he snapped closed his book and exited the train, along with other passengers, almost every one a student like himself. There was really no other reason to get off at this stop, Community College being only for the school and nothing else was in the vicinity of the college, as it was just off the highway.

He had a few minutes before his first class began so he went to a small café he frequented in building 'B' to get himself a coffee.

As he waited in line, he spotted a familiar face getting a pastry and a Red Bull.

"Hey, Lisa, what's up?"

"Oh hi, Shane," Lisa Richards said as she got in line one place behind him, a customer now between them. She was a bubbly blonde with a curvaceous figure and a pleasant smile. Though she was beautiful, she was a down home girl and never acted like her beauty deserved special treatment, which was what Shane found so attractive about her. They'd gone out on a few dates but nothing ever became serious, no doubt due to Shane still being hung up on Susan.

"Red Bull, huh? I never got into the stuff." He let the person behind him go next so he was standing with Lisa.

"Shit, Shane, I live off this stuff. You know how it is; cramming all night and with work, there's no time to sleep."

Shane only nodded. Actually, he didn't know how it was. His college was paid for from the money his mother got from the death of his father overseas. Because of it, he didn't have to work to pay his way through college.

He was next in line and he paid for his coffee and then decided to pay for Lisa's items, too.

"Thanks, Shane, that's real nice of you."

"Happy to do it," he smiled. "I guess you could call this a date then, huh?"

She shrugged. "If you like."

"I have some time before my class begins. Wanna hang out for a few minutes?"

"Sure, love to," she said.

They left the café and crossed the lobby to where there were tables for the students to relax between classes. The area was about half-full, most of the students reading or listening to music through their earbuds connected to their various electronic devices.

"So..." she began.

"So," Shane repeated.

There was an odd moment of silence between the two of them, where they both concentrated on their drinks, then Lisa said, "Have you heard about all the attacks going on?"

Shane shook his head.

"Really? It's been on the news almost all the time."

"No, I haven't had much time to watch TV lately."

"Well, you need to. People have been going crazy for some reason, mugging and trying to kill others. It's fucking wild. I heard that a few of the people who were attacked were even killed."

That made Shane think of Tim and he quickly told Lisa what had happened to his friend.

She slapped the table with her hand, making their drinks jump. "See? That's what I'm talking about. Someone attacked your friend, I'm sorry to say."

"Have they said why this is happening?" he asked.

She shook her head, her hair caressing her face. She brushed it away with a hand. "No, no one knows though you know there's always those talking heads on the news trying to figure the shit out. They just guess till they know more. I heard a lot of different things, everything from some kind of mass psychosis to terrorists putting something in the water. They don't know. They're all a bunch of assholes, if you ask me."

They talked for a bit more and then Shane checked his watch. "I have to get to class in building C."

"Yeah, me to. Want to walk together?" she asked.

"Sure that would be great," he replied and the two set off for the adjoining building.

Chapter 10

The Bunker Hill Community College complex was small, consisting of four main buildings, A, B C, E, that were all interconnected. As a stepping stone to larger colleges, it was simple in its design and function.

Building E was the library and gym, the A building was the theatre—for shows from the drama class—and B and C had decent-sized rooms for the classes, about the size of an average high school classroom. There was no building D, which Shane always found odd but not enough to query about.

It was the first class of the day so the college wasn't too crowded, but in time it would be full of bustling students from all walks of life, all trying to get an education and better themselves.

With Shane in the lead, he and Lisa rounded a corner to the next corridor and Shane promptly stopped in his tracks.

"Hey, what's wrong?" Lisa asked and then she had to stifle a scream, her hand going to her mouth.

Down the hall, about twenty feet, on the floor, was a student and a teacher. The identity of the student couldn't be seen but Shane recognized the teacher instantly. It was Professor Brown. He was a big man, well over six feet tall, with large hands and biceps. In many ways, Prof. Brown looked like he should have a job working construction than as a teacher.

At the moment, Prof. Brown was face deep in the stomach of the student, tearing at his victim's insides as if he was a rabid dog.

Through the blood covering Prof. Brown's face, Shane could see that the man's complexion was now very pale, some of his skin seeming to be sagging, as if it was rotting away on his face by the second. His eyes were pale and milky white, as if the man had bad cataracts. His pants were ripped below the knees, scratches embedded in his skin, and when Shane took a step closer, he saw that the professor had a wound on his neck. It looked a lot like a bite wound. So the teacher attacking the student had in kind been attacked by someone else.

Lisa couldn't control herself and she let out a high-pitched scream. Professor Brown's head snapped up and he swiveled his head until he was looking right at Shane and Lisa. He got to his feet and began moving towards them, dripping blood behind him in his wake, still chewing on a piece of intestine. He made a low groaning sound.

That was enough for Shane. He snatched Lisa's hand, turned, and dashed down the hallway, wanting to get as far away from Professor Brown as he could.

Chapter 11

Shane's eyes scanned the walls as he ran past them, Lisa's hand tugging at his a little. She kept begging him, pleading for him to stop.

"Shane! I can't keep running! We need to…"

"No, Lisa!" Shane snapped, pulling her harder, and then running again. She flailed her free arm to try and get away. "Lisa, if we stop, who knows what will happen? You saw Professor Brown!"

"I know but…Shane!" Lisa suddenly screeched, and Shane came to a sudden halt with her. At the end of the hallway, blocking their path, was Mr. Rodriguez, another professor.

Mr. Rodriguez had a bright personality and a way with the girls in his classes. He was handsome with a thin mustache and always had a smile for everyone. But this Mr. Rodriguez looked far different from the one Shane knew.

The man's black hair was a mess, and patches of his scalp was bleeding in places. The skin on his face was torn to ribbons and was now hanging from the sides of his head. His skin, once a dark tan, was now pale, with splotches of discolored veins crisscrossing his arms; his hands were grasping empty air as he raised them towards Lisa and Shane. One of his arms was bent unnaturally, as if it was broken, but the man didn't seem to mind. His mouth hung open, the slack jaw exposing his teeth. What used to be his prize-winning smile was now a horrible sight to behold.

"Mr. Rodriguez?" Lisa cried out in horror at the bloody man before her. With tears welling up in her eyes as fear overtook her, she walked towards him.

She'd always had a slight crush on him, as did many other female students that had him for a teacher.

"Lisa! Get away from him!" Shane cried out as Mr. Rodriguez moved closer to her. She didn't appear to hear him, her eyes locked on the bloody creature before her.

"Damn it, Lisa, come back here!" Shane yelled and was going to run to her and grab her but he could already see it was too late.

Mr. Rodriguez was middle-aged and of average build but had yet to let age make him weak or flabby. He pounced on Lisa, his hands grabbing her shoulders in a vice-like grip. They fell against a door that led into a classroom, where Shane heard the sounds of fighting and the screams from other students as the couple fell into their midst. Shane made a move toward the door, and suddenly six more people, all of them no longer human by the looks of them, came around a corner and charged him. Seeing he couldn't help Lisa, and that his own life was in peril, he did the only thing a rational person could do given the circumstances.

He ran for his life.

Upon reaching the quad, Shane saw more people running and screaming and he turned and dashed to building E, which was where the gym was located.

When he reached the gym, sports equipment was scattered everywhere. He made a sharp left, avoiding someone coming right at him, and ran into the men's locker room.

He snatched up a baseball bat and flipped it over, then spun around and stood in a batter's stance, staring at the door. He used to play baseball, but never truly liked it. Now he was hoping he could recall how to follow through on a swing. He might need to after all. His breathing came in ragged gasps, his heart thumping in his chest.

He'd never been so scared in all his life. He tried to imagine what his father would do if he was in this situation. Unfortunately, his father's voice was silent, leaving Shane to deal with this tenuous situation on his own.

Another professor came stumbling into the locker room. One look at the man and Shane knew he wasn't normal. As the man came at him, Shane closed his eyes and swung the bat for all he was worth. He felt the bat hit flesh and vibrate in his hands, then heard a thud and a snapping sound.

Shane opened his eyes to see the man standing in front of him, his arms stretched forward but no working brain to control them. The bat had left a large dent in his skull. Then the body sagged to the floor as blood pooled on the tiles.

Shane felt his stomach heave at the sight and he threw up, splashing his shoes as he bent over, gagging. He'd killed someone and the reality was too much to take.

But he didn't get much time to take in what he'd done as more bloody students and faculty spilled into the locker room. A quick headcount told Shane there were more than ten people in all. Most were strong males and one of them was the football coach. All had massive wounds on their bodies, their throats torn out. All had the same pale complexions and white eyes.

Shane felt faint. He tried to accept what was happening; it was like some bizarre horror movie and he had to wonder if he was in his bed at home sleeping and this was all a nightmare.

There were too many to fight and he ran farther back into the locker room. In the very back of the room was a red and white sign signifying it as an EXIT. Seeing this, he ran for the door. He wanted out all right, but would he make it before he was caught?

He was only a few feet from the door when a woman stepped out from behind an aisle of lockers and into his path.

It was another of the faculty, one of the guidance counselors, a Mrs. Simmons. Her complexion was pale and one of her eyes was missing, only a gaping dark socket looking back at Shane.

She had a jagged wound on her neck, and blood covered the front of her blouse. She was missing one shoe and stood slightly at an angle. Shane really liked Mrs. Simmons. He thought she was pretty and even had a small crush on her. She was only twenty-three after all; she wasn't much older than him.

"Mrs. Simmons?" Shane said, his voice cracking. "What happened to you?"

For a reply she lunged at him. He took a step backwards, but when he realized he was being followed by the others that had entered the locker room, he knew he had to go forward. Shoving Mrs. Simmons out of the way, he sent her sprawling across the floor into the path of his pursuers, then charged the door.

Immediately, an alarm went off overhead. It was a fire door of course.

He turned around and tried to close the door, but no sooner did he do this than an arm was jammed through the opening, the hand trying to grasp Shane. Using his shoulder, he attempted to push the door closed but there were simply too many bodies on the opposite side.

Deciding he needed to cut and run, he shoved one last time, then let it go and ran for his life. Behind him, the door slammed open and more zombies fell through the doorway.

By this time, Shane was long gone.

Chapter 12

As Shane ran for his life through the quad, he began to hear screams and yells and frightened voices as the undead faculty and students came out of the school to attack more people.

All the panicked cries of Shane's gradating class intensified as they were run down and savaged. The domino effect was in full force here and wherever a student was killed, that person would soon rise to join the attackers. It was utter madness.

The real panic set in when a car exploded out on the highway that bordered the college, then another and another. Sirens could be heard and then gunshots.

As smoke rose into the sky over building E, Shane stood aghast, not understanding how things could fall apart so quickly.

Unknown to Shane, some students had tried to escape by running into the small cafeteria in building E. Once there, panicked mistakes had been made which led to a ruptured gas line near one of the ovens.

As the cafeteria blew up, the fire began to spread throughout the building. More people began to panic, as windows were blown out to spray glass across the quad. Flames reached out of windows and smoke curled into the air, all to the sound of people screaming.

Shane stood frozen, staring back at his college as it burned. Bloody people were everywhere and even when one came right up to him, he still didn't move. At the last second, the bloody attacker turned away from Shane when movement to the left caught the zombie's eye. Spinning, the creature went after a screaming girl who had arrived at the college that day to scope it out.

Snapping out of his stupor, Shane ran away and finally slowed to a stop and leaned against a tree at the edge of the quad when he believed he was safe. Looking back, he saw more people coming from the direction of the subway, and as he studied them more closely, he realized they didn't look so hot. Blinking back tears, he shook his head to wake from this living nightmare.

Twenty feet away, he heard another scream and the sound of a small motor. Turning to see what it was, he spotted a man on a small red scooter get knocked off the machine by a group of bloody people. The student had blonde hair and a small belly from playing too many video games, but still looked young and healthy. He tried to fight back as he was forced to the ground, the rear tire of the scooter still spinning.

He never had a chance.

The people dove in with teeth and fingernails, ravaging the poor bastard like they were a pack of hungry wolves. The student fought back valiantly, punching and kicking, but the blows were ineffectual, as if the people felt no pain.

Soon, the screams faded as the zombies gorged themselves on the student's insides.

Shane wasn't looking at the dead student, but instead was staring at the scooter, which lay ignored a few feet from the crowd of feeding people. He knew he wasn't going to take the subway home, not with so much happening around him. The scooter would be perfect. But it was awfully close to the crowd and one mistake on his part would have him joining the original scooter's owner in death.

He studied the dozen or so people that were surrounding the dead scooter rider, trying to figure out who they were. It was a mix of the faculty and students. Each one was bleeding, some with torn body parts and organs hanging out, all with pale eyes that seemed to absorb the sunlight.

50

Lisa was among them, her bloody face seeming to be twisted into a smirk. In the background, more sirens could be heard as emergency services raced to the college and the accidents or the highway.

Shane made his move and began running to the scooter. A professor moving faster than the others spotted him and tried to cut him off, moaning loudly.

Shane dodged the man and kept running, reaching the scooter in seconds.

Picking it up, he jumped onto it and gunned the throttle. The small machine lurched forward but not fast enough for him to avoid being grabbed by another attacker.

Screaming in terror, he sent a wild punch at his attacker, feeling his hand hit the bone in the woman's face. Then he was free of the grip and moving down the thin road that led to the highway, picking up speed with each second. The scooter could go 50mph easily.

He risked a look in the handlebar mirror and he didn't like what he saw. People everywhere, some on the ground while others were over them, all covered in blood, the college in flames, sounds of carnage everywhere.

With tears in his eyes, he aimed the scooter to the highway and home. He needed to get there, to reach his mother, and together the two of them could figure things out.

As he drove, the tears in his eyes drying from the wind, he wished for the thousandth time that his father was alive to be with him.

Chapter 13

By the time he reached the neighborhood of his home, the streets were filled with the same tableaux as back at the college. It was hard to believe what he was seeing, and he still could barely wrap his head around it.

It appeared that since that morning, the world had come unglued.

He barely took the time to put the scooter on its center stand upon arriving at his house. Running to the front door, at first he didn't give it much thought that the door was wide open, nor did he see the bloody handprints on the doorjamb.

"Mom! Mom, where are you?" he called out as he ran into the house, then stopped at the stairs leading to the second floor.

There was mud on the stairs…and blood. The small table near the front door had been knocked over and there were more bloody footprints. Though his heart was beating a mile a minute, he finally paused long enough to take in the scene around him.

When he glanced to the right, to the opening to the kitchen, he could see there was spilled food on the floor and at least one chair had been knocked over. When he looked to the left, he could see into the living room and there, also, was disarray. It was like a bull had come charging into his house and had destroyed everything.

Outside, through the open front door, he heard yelling and what sounded like gunshots. What was going on at the college was happening here in his neighborhood, too, and he needed to get his mother so the two of them could leave. Where they would go wasn't at the front of his mind. He was in fight or flight mode and at the moment he only wanted to pick flight.

A low moan came to his ear and it was really close, like in the next room close. Taking a few steps closer to the living room, he paused at the doorway and peered into the room. The curtains on all the windows were wide open, with the exception of the one facing the street. That one had been torn down, as if someone had grabbed it, and when they were yanked back, the curtain had come with them.

There was the sound of mastication, and Shane thought of a cow chewing its cud, but he couldn't see where the noise was coming from.

As his eyes took in the room, he realized that the only place the sound could be coming from was behind the couch, which was hidden from his view.

Slowly, he took a step forward, then another.

By the time he'd taken three steps, he saw a foot, the owner lying supine on the floor. He recognized the shoe on the foot. It belonged to his mother.

"Mom, are you okay?" he asked, hesitant to step closer though he knew he had to. If his mother was hurt, he needed to help her. But after everything he'd seen, he was trepidatious. But still, his mother needed help and he could hear his father's voice in the back of his head, telling him to man up and get moving.

Standing taller, he rallied his courage and went to the edge of the couch, and looked down at something he thought he would only see in his worst nightmares.

His mother was lying dead on the floor, her eyes blank and open, staring at nothing. Her mouth hung slack, her head tilted to the side. Over her, digging into her stomach and pulling out ropes of greasy entrails, was their neighbor, Mr. Robinson.

Shane only took half a second to look at Mr. Robinson but he immediately saw that the man was like the people at the college. Mr. Robinson turned his head to look at Shane who saw that the man's eyes were the same milky white as the others he'd seen.

Shane took a step backwards in shock, as he tried to come to grips that his mother was dead, murdered by Mr. Robinson.

The zombie rose from Shane's mother, a large rope of intestine hanging from his mouth, and he began to move towards Shane, who was still frozen in terror. Shane stayed that way even when Mr. Robinson reached out with his blood-covered hand and wrapped them around Shane's throat and began squeezing.

Tears welled up in Shane's eyes as he looked at his mother dead on the floor. What was the point? Everyone he loved was dead.

Mr. Robinson kept squeezing, and then slowly leaned his face in to take a bite out of Shane's cheek.

And that was when Shane heard his father's voice in his head, yelling. *Run Shane, get out of here! You need to fight, son, you need to live! Don't give up!*

Snapping out of it, Shane reached out for a lamp on a table to his right and brought it up and smashed the base of it against Mr. Robinson's temple. The man stumbled backwards from the blow but it barely slowed him down.

Shane put the couch between him and the zombie and tried to figure out what to do next. And that was when he felt someone grab his ankle and he looked down to see his mother was on her side, pulling herself across the floor to reach him, her insides spilling out of her gaping abdomen to splash across the floor.

"Mom? It…it can't be. You're dead."

His mother opened her mouth and let out a low moan, her eyes pale and milky white. Shane gazed into those empty orbs and saw nothing of his mother. Whatever was at his feet wasn't the woman who had given birth to him, cared for him and loved him more than any other person on the planet.

No, he knew then that his mother was gone and by doing this, was able to grasp ever so slightly what was going on and what was happening to people.

But he couldn't hurt his mother, no matter what condition she was in. As Mr. Robinson rounded the couch, Shane jumped over it and landed in the middle on the center cushion. From there he jumped off to the floor and ran to the front door and back outside, slamming the door behind him.

Upon returning outside, he saw there were more people that didn't look too friendly on the street. As the door slammed, the people turned to see him and began moving towards Shane. His eyes went to the scooter, he realized there would be no time to get on it, start it, and try to escape before the people were on him. So, turning to the right, he dashed around his house and ran into his backyard, the horde right behind him.

Two dozen creatures were following closely, and he stopped suddenly when he realized he's reached a dead end. His yard was surrounded by a flat, white seven foot vinyl fence with no protuberances for him to use to climb over it.

He heard more moaning and spun around to find the horde closing in.

He was trapped! Then he took in the objects in the yard, such as chairs and a BBQ grill, and he did some quick math in his head. He'd found a way out.

He dashed for the chairs, jumped on one, then leaped two feet to the grill, and with it threatening to topple, he lunged for the top of the fence, his arms wrapping around the top as his body slammed against it.

With his feet kicking empty air, he pulled himself up and over, dropping down into his neighbor's yard. A Chihuahua began yapping at him and he stopped himself from kicking it like football, the annoying rat dog making more noise than the zombies.

Stepping over the dog, he ran out of the yard, into the next street, and kept on running.

Chapter 14

Shane ran right to Susan's house, wanting to make sure she was all right, and if not, hopefully he could help her.

The street around her house was in a similar state to his, with people running around while others attacked them. A man four houses down from Susan's was on his front lawn, shooting at anyone who came close.

A police squad car arrived and the man and the police got into a shootout before the man was killed. But he wasn't shot in the head, and moments after falling to the ground dead, he was back up again. Shocked at the man's imperviousness to bullets, the police shot him again and only when one of the bullets hit the man in the head did he stay down for good.

Shane couldn't believe it all. It was like the world was crumbling before his very eyes. His father had told him that civilization was fragile, like a house of cards, and one strong wind was all it would take to knock the entire thing over and smash it to rubble.

The house next to Susan's was burning and the flames were already reaching out through the roof, the acrid smoke tickling the back of his throat and making him want to cough. No fire services were in sight, the fire raging unchecked.

Shane ran to Susan's house and rang the doorbell five times, barely letting go of the button between rings. He tried to open the door but it was locked and though he rang the bell again and again, no one showed up. But he had nowhere else to go so he went around to the back door and tried to get in that way, but that door was locked, too.

An explosion ripped through the neighborhood from the street behind him, and Shane ducked his head out of instinct. When he looked into the horizon, he saw a large billowing gray cloud.

Deciding he had no choice about what to do next, he used his elbow and broke one of the small glass panes that made up the upper half of the back door. Careful not to cut himself, he reached inside and unlocked the door, then stepped into the kitchen.

The instant he stepped inside, he heard the distinct yet muffled sound of a scream and knew immediately it was from Susan. She sounded terrified.

"Susan? It's Shane! Where are you?" There was no reply, but as he moved deeper into the house, he heard the sound of banging, as if multiple fists were pounding on a wooden door.

As Shane entered the living room, he looked down on the floor to see two bodies, and when he moved closer, he saw that one of them was Dean. His throat had been torn out and his head had been cracked open, the brains leaking out to soak into the carpet. The other body was of a man in his forties, but the face was un-known to him, and Shane assumed it was one of the people out-side, who had gotten into the house, and Dean had tried to fight him off and had lost. There was a fire poker still embedded in the corpse's skull and Shane went and retrieved it. He took a second to wipe off the bits of brain matter stuck to the end of the poker on the corpse's pants.

He shook his head as he gazed down at his rival for Susan's affection. Though many times he'd wished Dean dead, Shane had never really wanted it to come to pass. But now here Dean was…very, very dead.

Another scream came to his ears and he looked up, realizing it was coming from the second floor. Then he heard more pounding.

Only thinking of Susan and not for himself, he dashed up the stairs and stopped cold on the second floor landing.

At the end, where Susan's bedroom was located, her door closed, stood both her parents. Mom and Dad were covered in blood and looked as if they'd been mauled by wild animals. Their eyes looked the same as others he'd seen—pure white orbs with no color.

The second Susan's parents spotted Shane, they stopped banging on the bedroom door, turned, and came at him, their hands reaching out to grab him.

He wanted to run away, to get as far from these two zombies as possible, but his love for Susan made him stand and fight, though he felt like he was going to shit himself at any moment, due to the terror filling him.

Dad was first, and with a low moan he lunged at Shane, who jumped back with a yell, and swung the poker with his eyes closed. He felt it hit meat and bone and opened his eyes to see the poker now stuck in Dad's head. As he yanked it back, Dad's hair and a small bit of brain matter came with it, but Dad was still going strong. Dad grabbed his arm and tried to bite him and Shane swung the poker again one-handed. This time it went in deeper into the same wound and a wet squelch could be heard as Dad's brain was penetrated. Dad slumped to the floor, dead for good.

Behind Dad, Mom was hungry and not at all perturbed that her undead husband had been killed in front of her. With a moan of her own, she charged at Shane, her hands opening and closing, her mouth moving up and down, as if she was trying to say something but couldn't get out the words.

Shane felt braver against Mom, as she was a small woman no more than five feet tall. Using the poker like a sword, he stabbed her in the chest. She didn't die but she was held at arm's length, and Shane fought to keep her away from him as she snapped her teeth and reached for him.

Backing up to the stairs, he swung her around and let her fly off the landing. She went into the air and then gravity took over, and she plummeted down each step, ass over elbows until she stopped in a heap of limbs at the bottom. Her right leg was broken, as was her left arm, but Mom barely seemed to notice and quickly rolled onto her stomach and tried to crawl up the stairs. Like an inchworm, she struggled but was making no headway. Shane watched her for a full thirty seconds, and seeing she wasn't going to be getting to the second floor anytime soon—if ever—he turned and ran to Susan's bedroom door.

"Susan, it's me, Shane. It's safe now. You can come out."

Before he knew what was happening, the door was thrown open and Susan was jumping into his arms. "Oh my God, Shane, my parents went crazy after they got home," she said into his ear as she hugged him. "They said something about getting attacked by some homeless man and that they didn't feel well. They went to lie down in their bedroom. A few hours later I went to check on them and they tried to attack me. My dad grabbed me but I got away and I barely made it to my room before he got me again. What the hell is going on?"

"I don't know," he said, keenly aware of her breasts pushed up against his chest. He knew this wasn't the time to get aroused but he found his pants growing tighter despite himself. "I think it's the same thing that happened to Tim."

She pushed herself away from him and looked around. "Wait, where are my parents?"

Shane swallowed the knot in his throat and pointed to her prone father lying at the end of the hallway.

"Shit, Susan, I'm really sorry I had to kill your dad," he said apologetically. "But he tried to kill me first."

Susan began to cry and she went to her father. She reached out to touch him but stopped at the last second. "Where's my mom?"

Shane frowned, not wanting to tell her what he'd done to her mom. He walked over to Susan and then pointed down the stairs to where her mother was still trying to crawl up the steps. She hadn't done much since Shane left her. Not so much as climbed one step.

"She came at me and I threw her down the stairs. She's pretty fucked up but, hey, at least she's not dead." He smiled wanly, trying to be positive.

"At least she's not d…" Susan began and trailed off, amazed that Shane would even say such a thing.

A car crash outside caused Shane to snap out of his present situation and look at the bigger picture. He could smell smoke, too, as it wafted into the house. The home next door was nothing but a blazing inferno and if he knew if they stayed in Susan's house, it was possible the fire would spread to her house, too. He knew they had to get away.

He decided not to tell her about Dean being dead; she had enough to worry about at the moment. After quickly explaining about the burning home next door and the chaos going on outside, Susan seemed willing to leave, though she was mostly in a daze from the death of her father and the mutilation of her mother.

"My…my parents' car is in the driveway, we can take that," she said, staring at her mother's mangled body as the woman tried to climb up the stairs. Mom's mouth opened and closed, the teeth clacking on empty air like a pair of walking teeth that clattered with each step the toy made.

"Okay, where are the keys?" he asked.

"In…in the kitchen." She pointed down the stairs and to the right, where the doorway leading to the kitchen was located.

"Good, follow me," he said and began walking down the stairs. They had to step over Susan's mother to reach the kitchen. He led the way, taking the steps slowly. A few steps below, Mom hissed and snapped her teeth. She accidentally caught her tongue between her teeth and bit off the tip. Blood pooled in her mouth to drip out the sides, to then splatter on the closest steps.

When Shane was only three steps in front of Mom, he stopped and turned to face Susan, who was crying again.

"Oh God, Shane, what's wrong with her? Why is she acting like that?"

"I don't know, but whatever it is, it's not just her. Your dad was the same way and the people outside have gone fucking nuts. It's the entire city, maybe even the state. Okay, so we have to jump over your mom to leave here. Can you do that?" he asked.

"I...I guess so," she whispered as she stared at her mother, who now resembled a wounded wild animal. The eyes were the hardest to look at. They were bone white, even the irises were milky. Susan thought about the saying of how the eyes were gateways to the soul. If that was so than her mother had no such thing anymore.

"Good, you go first and I'll be right behind you. I promise."

She merely nodded, her eyes darting back to her mother. Susan walked down another step, her mom's reaching fingers only inches from Susan's feet. Susan was frozen and Shane knew she needed a push, so that's what he did. Susan screamed as she felt him shove her in the back and then she was jumping over her mom and landing on the floor just beyond her mother's feet. Mom turned to try and grab her but Susan was running to the kitchen a second later. She didn't look back.

Now it was Shane's turn.

Getting two steps away, he jumped over Mom. But he miscalculated and Mom was able to stretch up as Shane went over her and she managed to wrap one hand around his left ankle. Shane felt the tug as he was halted in mid-air and then he was falling face first to the floor. Putting his hands out before him, he saved himself from a broken nose and cried out in pain as his hands and arms took the brunt of the fall on the hardwood floor. Then he was flat on the floor, the wind knocked out of him.

Mom had pulled herself off the stairs and was crawling up Shane's body, her mouth dripping blood. She moaned louder, her eyes jumping in their sockets.

Shane shook his head to clear the fog that had descended and he rolled onto his side, looking down his body to see Mom coming for him. Her face was even with his crotch and he forced images of her deciding that was a good spot to begin feeding.

He scooted a few inches away and dragged her with him. Knowing he had to act fast, he pulled back his right foot as far as it would go, so that his knee touched his chest, then he kicked out with as much force as he could muster. The bottom of his sneaker connected with Mom's face, shattering her nose and sending bits of cartilage shooting into her brain. The bits of shrapnel did just enough damage to fry her brain, and though not fully dead, she lost some motor skills and let go of Shane's leg, her face contorting into what looked to Shane like a mask of pain.

Pushing her away from him with his foot yet again, he crawled away a few feet and stood up, though a wave of dizziness rushed over him as he got to his feet. He stumbled into the kitchen, where Susan was waiting for him.

"Let's get out of here," he said. The kitchen was full of smoke from the burning home next door, thanks to an open window. More explosions could be heard coming from a nearby street. Things were deteriorating fast outside.

Susan held up the keys to her parents' car and tossed them to Shane. There was a small white rabbit's foot on the chain.

With Shane leading the way, they ran into the backyard and then to the front of the house. By the time they reached the street, both were coughing heavily from smoke inhalation. Susan was practically on her knees as she gagged and tried to find her breath. The street was filled with smoke, a rolling cloud that made it hard to see. Shane stopped halfway to the car when he realized she wasn't behind him. Turning to see where she was, he saw three shapes appear out of the smoke and jump her. Susan began to scream as she was forced to the ground.

"Susan, no!" Shane yelled and began to run to her, but before he was halfway there another shape came out of the smoke and tackled him, the keys in his hand flying out of his grip to land in the nearby bushes. He dropped face first into the grass that made up the front lawn. The smell of the soil and grass filled his sinuses and he kicked out with his right leg. Feeling his foot hit something solid, he quickly got to his feet to continue racing to Susan.

But as he began again, he stopped after taking three steps, seeing it was too late to save her.

The three figures were covering her in a dog-pile and only her right arm and leg could be seen clearly. The fingers twitched spastically as the three figures tore her apart. Her screams were mercifully cut short when her throat was torn out.

A low moan from behind him told Shane his attacker that had tackled him was coming again. Shane's head went back and forth to the stumbling zombie and Susan, not able to decide what to do.

He was frozen in place, but then he heard his father's voice, telling him that to retreat was his only option, that Susan was gone, he could do nothing for her.

With more shapes appearing out of the roiling smoke, Shane heeded his father's voice and began to run away from the terrible scene of carnage. He had to dodge between reaching shapes in the smoke, but he was too fast and soon the smoke was gone and he was running full speed down the middle of the street. Tears filled his eyes, causing the world to become blurry.

Susan was dead, just like his mother, and Lisa. Every time he tried to help someone they died. It was like he was cursed.

He ran for a full fifteen minutes until his side began to cramp and he had to stop and breathe. As he stood in the street, bent over, he saw more people nearby coming for him, but he had a second to catch his breath before he had to run away.

His mind raced with all that had happened and he knew he needed to go somewhere and rest, to take stock of everything, to try and figure out what to do next.

Once more his father's voice came to him and told him where he could go, where he'd be safe for at least a little while. He didn't argue with the voice, even if he wanted to, he was simply too mentally and physically exhausted to care.

With his side ache subsiding a little, he began to jog this time, his mind set on a destination.

Shane was gasping for air and his legs were sore by the time he reached his destination in the woods two miles from his home. It was a large shack in the middle of the forest used for hunting, about four feet by four feet. Openings were cut into all four sides and they could be opened like windows so that the hunter within could watch the woods but stay dry if it rained, as well as staying out of the wind. He charged inside after unlocking the combination on the door. Only then did he stop and bend over to catch his breath.

He sat in the small shack for hours, too scared to move and then, as the sun was setting, he heard footfalls outside. His heart in his throat, he peered through a crack in the wood slats to see if he could make out what was out there. A deer maybe? A raccoon? He couldn't see a thing.

Then the door began to rattle in its frame and Shane felt his legs go weak. This was it, one of them had found him. He was trapped, there was nowhere for him to run. He didn't give it much thought that the attacker was working the lock on the door, as he didn't know what the dead were capable of yet.

The door opened, the hinges creaking softly from rust, and then a flashlight beam hit Shane in the face. He screamed, raising his hands before him. "No, don't kill me! Leave me alone!"

"Shane? Relax, son, it's just me, it's fine. You're safe here."

Shane slowly calmed down, recognizing the voice immediately.

Taking his hands away from his face, the flashlight was lowered and Shane blinked as his eyes adjusted.

The person before him slowly took shape, and as he did, Shane felt relief flood through him.

Standing in the doorway with the flashlight in one hand and a hunting rifle in the other, a wide smile pasted on his face, was a hunting friend of his father's, a man who also used the shack to hunt.

"Mr. McAlister?" Shane said in amazement.

"That's right. It's just me, and I have to ask again, son. What's wrong with you? You look like the Devil himself was chasing you."

"You mean you don't know?" Shane asked.

"Know what?"

"About the crazy people…the *dead* people."

Mr. McAlister scratched his head in curiosity. "I've been out here for a few days hunting deer. Why, is something going on back in the city?"

Shane sat taller and waved the man inside with him. Then he began to tell his tale.

Chapter 15

Corporal Johnson limped down the street, feeling like he could sleep for a week.

Over the past day and a half, he had traveled mostly on foot, as all around him civilization seemed to be crumbling. The buses had stopped and there were no cabs to be found and he couldn't steal a car as he didn't know how to hotwire one. He knew it wasn't as easy as they made it out on television, not with new cars having anti-theft guards and the like.

No one would pick him up when he waved for them to stop, not that he blamed them. A man in an army uniform, covered in blood and armed, wasn't a reassuring image. Finally, he stole a bicycle from a front yard and was able to make better time, and now, his destination was only a few blocks away.

The hospital was at the end of the street, the parking lot full of vehicles, many parked carelessly, some not parked at all, with doors hanging open. The sky was overcast, and as he got closer, he saw people rushing about, as well as countless ambulances and a few police cars.

The previous night, Johnson slept in a car he'd found unlocked. As he'd slept, he'd had terrible nightmares that caused him to toss and turn in the back seat.

In the dream, he'd been walking through the forest and then heard a noise behind him. He peered around, and spotted shapes sitting at the edge of a lake, drinking. They didn't seem to notice him or if so, they didn't care. He continued to watch the creatures, curious as to what they were.

Then he noticed that the water was dyed blood-red, and full of pale, bloodied bodies. The creatures had milky-white eyes that glowed in the darkness, but that was all Johnson could see. Then one of the creatures looked up, spotted him, and the group all came at him at once, each one trying to be the first to reach him. Johnson saw their stomachs were bloated, their flesh peeling and desiccated, their bones protruding from their cracked flesh in places.

Turning, he ran, and though he was fast, they were always right behind him, dancing between the trees. Finally, he scurried up a tree to escape his pursuers. The creatures looked up at him from the bottom of the tree, their pale eyes glowing, and they surrounded him. Immediately, Johnson could smell their foul odor of rot and decay waft up to him and it made him want to vomit. They lunged at the base of the tree, scratching at the trunk with claw-like hands, and Johnson let out a yell in fear, knowing what would happen to him if he was to be dislodged from his perch. The entire tree shook as they struck the tree again and again. Leaves rained down around him, but he held fast to the tree branch he was on. Finally, the creatures gave up and they wandered away.

The rest of the night was filled with less haunting dreams, though many just as vivid. But every time Johnson thought of the dream with the creatures with pale eyes, a chill went down his back and he began to sweat. It had seemed so real.

Despite how tired he was, he kept riding the bike to the hospital. A wave of exhaustion flooded through him and once more he desperately wanted to sleep. He shook himself awake, realizing he was drifting off.

More people like the old man in the farmhouse were seen roaming the street. They chased fleeing people, but Johnson was able to ride away when one tried to grab him. Infected was the word that came to mind. Something had infected the population with some kind of madness, one that did incredible things, things that couldn't be true. But he'd seen it for himself. He'd seen that farmer get up when the man had clearly been dead and Johnson had had to kill him a second time.

He realized he was fading again and shook himself awake, almost falling off the bicycle and landing in a muddy puddle pooling on the edge of a lawn thanks to the underground sprinkler system the house had. He thought that funny. The world seemed to be collapsing but the sprinklers went on as always.

Leaving the bike on the sidewalk, he walked through the cars in the hospital parking lot—now that he was closer he saw there were even more parked haphazardly—and approached the building. The side he was on had the Emergency Room entrance so he chose that as his destination. As he tried to enter, however, he saw that the lobby was filled with yelling, screaming people, all who wanted to receive medical attention. Not in the mood to wait, and brandishing his gun so that others could see, he shoved his way through the crowd until he was inside the lobby. People gave him a wide berth upon seeing his rifle and the blood covering him.

The hospital was a madhouse of activity. A nurse, seeing his uniform, came up to him and told him military and police officers got priority treatment. She quickly led him to a bed past a set of double doors where he could be helped. As he was led through the swinging double doors and they closed behind him, the noise from the lobby was immediately cut in half and Johnson sighed. At least now he could hear himself think a little

The nurse was around thirty, with a kind smile and red hair. Her eyes were hazel, and Johnson found that he liked being lost in her eyes. Though exhausted, he found himself becoming attracted to her, despite the fact that she was barely looking at him. In fact, no sooner had she put him in one of the few remaining empty beds, than she was off again to help someone else. As he looked around, he saw more people, each one looking in pretty rough shape. He heard some of the conversations in passing and the gist was that most of the people in the Emergency Room had either been in accidents or were attacked by others or worse. Gripping his rifle tighter, he made sure it was close to him. It was all he had to keep himself safe.

Johnson didn't wait long, and as he stared at the other patients, he looked up to see a frazzled-looking doctor coming towards him, the man peeling off a pair of bloody gloves to put on a fresh set.

The doctor was an average-looking man, around fifty-years-old, with gray hairs touching his dark black hair on the sides. A few more wrinkles were on his distressed face than were no doubt there at the beginning of his shift.

"Hello there, son, I'm Dr. Whitfield. Can you tell me exactly what's wrong with you? Is any of the blood on you yours?"

Johnson shook his head slowly and tried to stand up, but when he did, a wave of exhaustion flooded through him and he grew lightheaded. He tried to speak, but couldn't, then said, "I don't know, I kinda feel…"

Before he could say more, he slumped back to the bed, unconscious.

Chapter 16

Dr. Whitfield stabbed a needle into Johnson's arm, injecting him with a stimulant. More spent needles lay on a tray next to him, from other patients injected as well.

The doctor pulled out a small flashlight from a pocket and pried open one of Johnson's eyelids to examine the pupil. "Nurse! This man has fainted. It looks like he's suffered a concussion, too. And he looks dehydrated. Set up an IV drip."

She nodded, running back out of the room, and returning seconds later with an IV bag. She connected the IV to Johnson's arm. Another IV was connected as well. She took a moment to remove Johnson's shoes, dropping them on the floor. She was going to take the rifle from the bed but then left it, not wanting to touch the firearm.

"Is that all, Doctor?" she asked upon finishing.

Dr. Whitfield nodded acknowledgement. "You did well, nurse. Go back to your other patients." He looked around the room. "Which there are many."

Dr. Whitfield knew the nurse well. Her name was Tammy and she was twenty-two-years-old. She was slim and athletic with pert breasts that made the doctor feel far too old for his age.

She nodded her head, her blonde hair falling over her shoulders, as she looked at the doctor to make sure there was nothing else he needed. After a few moments of hesitation, she turned and walked out of the room.

He admired her shapely figure as she left. "So young," Dr. Whitfield sighed, smirking. He removed his surgical gloves, putting them in the waste container. Johnson was laying still, his mouth open slightly. The doctor's eyes went to the rifle as well but he left it next to the sleeping soldier. The way things were going in the hospital, it was possible the man was going to need it. The soldier would be fine, he just needed a few hours of rest.

The loudspeaker overhead began to chant his name, someone paging him to yet another crisis.

He shook his head, sighing heavily. Where the hell was the CDC? He'd called them hours ago. There was something happening to the population, an infection of some kind and he was ill equipped to handle it, and so was the hospital. But despite this, he'd given an oath to help the sick and wounded and that was what he was going to do, no matter how hopeless it seemed

He left Johnson's bedside, rushing away, where another patient had been attacked while outside and was bleeding badly.

Many hours later, Dr. Whitfield was finally allowed to go home after more than thirty-six hours straight on call. He was exhausted, but he couldn't wait to get home and see his family and get some much-needed rest.

The streets were filled with people driving like madmen and some running here and there, while others were wandering around aimlessly, their faces one of animalistic horror. He even saw a mugging—or what he believed was a mugging—the victim being jumped by two men. He didn't stop, but continued driving home. He'd tried calling 9-1-1 on his cell phone to report the attack but he couldn't get through. All lines were jammed. It made him think of the hospital and how full it was. The only reason he was able to leave at all was that he'd threatened to quit if he wasn't allowed to leave.

He parked in his driveway and quickly walked up to his front door, admiring the rose bushes lining the cement path. His wife took extra care of them and it showed.

Opening the front door and stepping inside, he called out, "Honey, I'm home!" to his wife, also hoping his two children would hear and come running like they usually did. The house was in darkness, only a dim light visible at the end of the hallway that led to the kitchen and living room. As he put down his briefcase, he thought he saw a small shadow cross by the feeble light.

"Tina, is that you?" he called out. Tina was his eight-year-old daughter, and she loved to hide and jump out and say, "Boo!" Her hair was a golden blonde and her eyes a lively blue. Her mind was always filled with new ideas and she was very bright for a girl her age.

He walked into the living room and found the television on, and on the floor watching it was Tina, and next to her was Billy, her brother.

Joey was a boy who knew no boundaries, especially for a seven-year-old. He loved Legos, toy cars, and cartoons and would watch hours of TV if allowed to. His dirty-brown hair was unbrushed. Dr. Whitfield smiled at his two children. He couldn't be more proud of them.

"It's late, you two, that's enough TV for one night. Get ready for bed now, please. Is your mother in bed already?" Without waiting for a reply, he turned off the television, and walked into the kitchen, flipped on the light, and opened the refrigerator to get something to drink. There was a plate on the counter covered in foil, and he knew his wife had made him dinner earlier in the hopes he would come home at a decent hour. It was tough being a doctor but he and his wife had made it work and he loved her more now than ever before.

Taking a beer from the refrigerator, he twisted off the top and drank half of it in one breath, relishing the taste. He could feel his exhaustion creeping up on him and knew he would sleep as soon as his head touched the pillow.

Looking at the entrance to the kitchen, he saw that Tina had entered. Her hair was hanging over her face and he couldn't see her visage too well. She walked over to him and hugged his leg. He reached down to hug her back.

And that's when he saw her open her mouth wide, her hair falling from her face to expose a countenance much like the ones he'd seen on people in the street on the way home. There was blood on her throat, the wound seeping dark liquid.

She tried to bite him, but her small teeth couldn't get past the material of both his pants and sock beneath. But he did feel the pressure of her teeth pushing on his skin. He watched in horror as his lovely daughter looked up at him and he saw that her once beautiful eyes were now pale and devoid of color, her complexion waxy and sickly. She let out a hiss that sent a chill down his spine, and he pushed her away. She fell onto her butt and then went to all fours like a wild animal. Behind her was Joey, his eyes the same, his mouth open, teeth bared to feed.

Dr. Whitfield took a step back, dropping his beer to the kitchen floor. The bottle didn't break, but rolled under the kitchen table, the remaining liquid spilling onto the tiles. In the back of his mind he thought that the spilled beer would anger his wife, that she would yell at him for it. Though thinking this was foolish given the circumstances, it was there nonetheless.

Turning, he crossed the kitchen to the back door, opened it, dashed through it, then slammed the door just as he felt the two small bodies of his children strike the door. He could hear them groaning as they scratched at it.

He stood there for a second, listening to them moan and hiss, and he felt tears welling up in his eyes.

Running around the house, he felt for the car keys still in his pocket and then stopped and looked up at the front of the house, something catching his eyes.

Upon arriving home, he had missed this, but now, standing at a different angle, he wondered how he could have ever not seen it when walking up the cement path.

As he gazed up to the second floor window that was for their shared bedroom, he saw his wife standing there.

She was covered in blood, her left cheek missing, and from such a short distance away, he could see that her wounds were from tiny teeth.

Her eyes were white, void of emotion. She began to slap on the window, moaning, wanting to break through, and finally the glass gave and she tumbled out of the window to land on her head, glass shards falling around her. There was a dull snap and the body slumped forward onto its stomach. It didn't move.

Dr. Whitfield bit back a scream of horror, then after a full minute of staring at his wife's body, he got back into his car, and with tears filling his eyes, began to drive.

Dr. Whitfield reached the intersection at the end of his street and took a right, then drove for three minutes before coming to a traffic light.

The light turned red and he stopped, waiting patiently for the light to turn green, as tears rolled down his cheeks. His lips trembled with sorrow and he wracked his mind on where to go next. Should he go to the police? It seemed like a sound idea.

His driver's side window was partially rolled down, and as he sobbed and tried to decide where to go, a man in a bloody business suit stepped off the sidewalk and headed towards the car.

Dr. Whitfield never saw the man, nor did he see the others that came at him from the passenger side. It was just as the light turned green, and he was about to go, that hands reached through the window and yanked him out of the car.

The zombies coming from the passenger side didn't have to walk around the car, as once the doctor was pulled from the driver's seat, the car began to roll forward, allowing them easy access to the man before them. The car rolled straight for almost a block before veering to the left and hitting a parked car.

Dr. Whitfield wasn't worried about his car, he was too busy dying.

Chapter 17

Corporal Johnson opened his eyes and looked around at his surroundings. He was in a hospital room, lying in bed.

He was cold and he looked down to see he was wearing a hospital gown. Only the air conditioner broke the silence. He lifted his blankets and saw that he seemed to be intact and the wounds he'd suffered in the helicopter crash had been cleaned and bandaged. Sitting up, he looked down at himself and realized he was going to be okay, despite the headache and aching muscles.

A doctor walked into the room minutes after he'd awoken. He was in his late sixties with blood splatter on his white coat and eyes that looked like they hadn't closed in days. Still, the man managed to flash Johnson a polite smile. "Good morning, young man, you have no idea how lucky you are! I'm Dr. Stevens. I've been assigned to your case."

Johnson sneered in distaste. "Lucky? I feel like I was run over by a truck?"

"Maybe, but you're alive and many in this hospital can't say the same. You're aware what's going on, aren't you?"

Johnson blinked at the man in reply.

"You're a soldier and you were wounded. Surely you've been out there fighting to stop all the attacks."

"I was in a chopper crash after leaving Hanscom Air Force base. I don't know much more than that. But I've seen how people have been acting firsthand." He tried to get off the bed but stopped when he felt lightheaded.

"Easy now, son, you have a concussion. You need to rest. I had you moved up here to a private room yesterday as we needed the bed down in Emergency. We're full to breaking right now."

"I need to get out of here and back to my unit. I need to report in," Johnson said and tried to get up, but his legs wouldn't work and he slumped to the floor. Dr. Stevens went to him and helped him back onto the bed.

"Maybe so, but you need to rest first. A concussion isn't anything to laugh at. It can be very serious. Look, I've been patching people up all day and I've sent many to the morgue, only once there, they haven't stayed dead."

"What?"

"I know it sounds crazy, but there's something happening, something where the dead won't stay dead."

"Doctor, you sound like we're actors in a horror movie."

"Perhaps, but sometimes life imitates art and all I know is that I've seen people die and then return to life personally, as hard as that is to swallow."

"Where's my rifle," Johnson asked as he looked around the room. Before the doctor could answer, though, screams sounded from the hallway outside, followed by people running by Johnson's room.

Dr. Stevens went to the door and stepped out into the hallway and walked down it until he reached the nurse's desk. As he looked into rooms within eyesight, he saw people wearing toe tags and little else, feeding on the patients in the beds. Blood was everywhere and screams filled the hospital. Turning, Dr. Stevens ran back to Johnson's room and quickly stepped back inside, slamming the door closed, his face filled with fear.

"What's wrong?" Johnson asked.

"Those people I told you about? The ones coming back to life? Well, they're coming this way."

Johnson got out of bed and went to the door. Opening it slowly, he peered into the hallway, only to slam the door and lean his back against it. "Shit, you weren't kidding." Images of what had happened to him at the farmhouse flooded his mind, then wisps of the dream he'd had tickled the edge of his brain. He turned to Dr. Stevens. "I need something to wear."

The doctor went to a cabinet and took out a pair of hospital scrubs and a pair of slippers left from the last patient to occupy the room. "Here, put these on. It's the best I can do at the moment."

Johnson got dressed quickly and when he was slipping on the last slipper said, "My rifle, where is it?"

Dr. Stevens shrugged. "I...I don't know, it should have been brought up here with you when you were moved to this room."

Johnson frowned. Some overeager nurse or doctor must have decided to take it for themselves, which now left Johnson unarmed. "We need to get out of here. Come with me."

"And the point of that would be what? From what I've heard on the radio and TV, those things are everywhere. There's nowhere to go."

Johnson put on a dazed expression. "What do you mean? There's always someplace to go! So what, you plan on just lying down and dying?"

Dr. Stevens shook his head. "No, of course not but I also don't want to be running all over the city. I'm not a brave man, I'm afraid. I wouldn't survive out there with things the way they are. It's chaos, martial law. No, I'll stay here until the police can regain control."

Johnson nodded. "And what if they don't? Listen to me. I've seen those things in action. You shoot them and they don't go down, they don't fear being hurt. Now, come with me or so help me I'll drag you behind me like a fucking child."

The doctor sighed heavily. "Fine. What do you need?"

"Well, transportation and weapons for one," Johnson said. "I had weapons when I came to the hospital."

"I don't know where your weapons are, but I have a jeep in the parking garage." He reached into his pocket and withdrew a keychain with six keys on it. "Here are the keys."

Johnson took the keys and pocketed them. "Good, we'll take that and I can figure out where to get a gun once we're away from here."

"Well, if they're not looted yet, there are gun shops in the area. There's one right on Broadway."

"Good idea. Okay, let's go. I'll lead."

They left the hospital room and went right to the fire stairs, and with people screaming and the moans of the dead following them, they moved down the stairs and made it to the parking garage without incident.

Dr. Stevens pointed out the jeep that was his and Johnson got into the driver's seat. Now that he was moving he had to admit he felt much better, though his head still hurt.

"Come on, Dr. Stevens! Get in the jeep!" Johnson yelled as he started the engine.

From around another parked car, four zombies popped up and tackled Dr. Stevens. He fell to the ground, screaming as they began to tear into him.

"Go!" he yelled at Johnson, punching one of his attackers in the face.

Gunshots sounded from nearby as well and a stray bullet hit the side mirror of the jeep. Saving the doctor was hopeless and whoever was shooting wasn't paying attention to what they hit so Johnson had no choice but to get out of there.

"Sorry, Doc, I tried."

With tires squealing on the cement, he raced out of the garage and into the street, the screams of Dr. Stevens fading away behind him.

Chapter 18

Shane stood in the middle of a gas station a few miles from his home, night having fallen hours ago and a new day about to dawn in less than an hour. The station was deserted with a big sign out front that said there was no gas. Anyone passing by would keep on going he hoped.

The power was out, and the glass doors and windows were shattered. There was a pool of blood on the floor and Shane tried not to think where the owner of that blood was right now. He thought of his mother and wondered where she was. Was she walking around out there killing people? Was she eating them, too?

He went to the counter and crouched behind it, then watched the street. Time passed slowly and then he heard someone walking on the crushed glass from the shattered glass door. A figure stepped inside the building, covered in blood and moaning. Its right leg was broken, the white of bone sticking out, its left arm hanging limp. Half of its face was scarred by burns.

Shane jumped over the counter, holding his weapon of choice, a can of bug spray and a cigarette lighter. Pressing the button on the top of the can, he ignited the spray, making a half-ass flame-thrower. The flames hit the zombie in the face. The body fell to the floor, its upper torso and face now nothing but charred flesh. While it burned, Shane quickly stabbed it with a long, metal rod taken from a display for motor oil and then dragged the corpse into the back with the rest of the bodies of the zombies he'd already taken down. The place was beginning to reek more and more every hour.

Over the last day, he had killed more than a dozen zombies, but his hideout wasn't safe anymore and today was the day he was going to move. He and Mr. McAlister had been planning to leave and head for the hills outside of town; there was a Kawasaki KZ250 motorcycle with a full tank of gas in the service bay waiting for him.

He was going to meet Mr. McAlister at the rear parking lot at the local shopping mall, then they would loot a store for food and weapons and head for the hills. Mr. McAlister was out searching for more supplies at the moment.

Shane had learned to ride a motorcycle years ago, having practiced on a dirt bike his dead friend Tim had owned. Now that skill was paying off. Looking outside, he saw that the sky was lightening and morning was coming. Checking his watch, he saw it was time to go and meet Mr. McAlister.

He went to the bay and walked to the motorcycle, climbed on it, and started it up. He'd been lucky when he found it lying on its side in the road, the keys still in the ignition. He didn't think about what had happened to the owner of the machine, nor had he paid attention to the dried droplets of blood on the seat.

Putting the bike into first gear, he rode out onto the street, avoiding a few slow walkers, then took off down the dark road. There was very little resistance in his way until he reached the shopping mall parking lot. He had to swerve around bodies that reached for him. He kicked a few out of his way and then reached the back of the mall, but the pickup truck Mr. McAlister had been driving was nowhere to be seen. Meanwhile, zombies were slowly walking his way, and if he stayed for too long, he was going to end up becoming trapped.

Checking his watch, he saw that Mr. McAlister was late, and he tapped his finger on the handlebar as he bit his lip nervously. Why were there so many zombies at the shopping mall? Were there people inside it? He tried to look over the heads of the crowd to see the glass doors of the shopping mall but he was too far away to make anything out.

Minutes passed and the zombies were far too close for comfort, then, deciding that he couldn't stay where he was, he drove away, only the zombies were too closely packed for him to make it safely. He gunned the engine and hit a body, knocking it over, but he almost lost his balance. If he fell off the bike, it was all over.

Hands reached for him, trying to pull him off the motorcycle and he lashed out, kicking as he drove in circles. His headlight lit up pale and bloody faces in the pre-dawn as he tried to break free. He planned on returning to the gas station, and once there, he would wait for Mr. McAlister to return. If he didn't then he would figure something out.

He spotted an opening in the crowd and took it, shooting forward, but at the last second, the gap was closed and he had to cut to the right, which sent him driving straight for the glass doors of the mall.

He was going too fast to stop and he crashed into one of the glass doors on the far right, the safety glass raining down around him as the motorcycle slid across the polished tiles. He rolled right behind it after falling off the seat.

As he came to a stop, people came out from where they'd been watching and quickly covered the door with plywood, and with an electric drill and sheet metal screws, they quickly secured the door so that the zombies couldn't get in, which was good, because in no time flat, fists were pounding on the wood as other zombies gathered around the other glass doors. Pale, bloody faces pushed up against the glass as the living dead tried to break in, but they weren't strong enough to penetrate the barrier.

Shane blinked as he lay on the floor, doing mental inventory of his body. Nothing felt broken.

He looked up to see a man standing over him.

"Nice entrance. You know, we would've opened the door for you, kid," the man said with a wry smile.

"Who're you?" Shane asked.

The man was in his mid-thirties, with light brown hair and an unshaven jaw, his body of medium build. He knelt down next to Shane and helped him sit up, then brushed some errant glass out of Shane's hair. "Welcome to the Seacrest Mall, kid. One stop shopping at it's best. Just don't ask anyone to help you carry your shit to your car, if you get what I mean."

"Oh stop it, Carl, you're confusing the boy," a woman Shane's mother's age said as she joined Carl. She was a plump woman wearing jeans and a yellow Winnie the Pooh sweatshirt taken from the Disney store. "Ignore Carl, dear, he likes to tease the new arrivals."

"Tease, hell, this kid almost got us all killed, Myra. If it wasn't for me who said he was gonna pull some action movie shit like he did, we wouldn't have been ready to cover that broken door."

"Yes, yes, Carl, we all know how wonderful you are," Myra said with a rolling of her eyes.

Behind Carl and Myra were standing forty to fifty more people. Half were men, the rest women and children, all of different ethnicities. All looked scared and exhausted and almost everyone was holding melee weapons of some sort.

Shane glanced around. "Who are you guys? What are you doing here?"

"I think I can answer that," another man said. He was in his late fifties, wearing a torn and blood-stained business suit. His dark brown hair, once neatly styled, was now a mess and looked as if it hadn't seen a comb in days. Under the emergency lights set at the corners of the mall's ceiling, his eyes locked on Shane, scanning him up and down. "I'm George Bartlett. I own a small Men's store here in the mall. Because of that I know this place better than most of the folks here, so I'm kind of the leader of our little ragtag group. What's your name, son?"

"I say we call him Evel Knievel," Carl joked. A few laughed, but not many. The zombies glaring at everyone at the doors had a way of dampening the mood.

"I'm Shane. Shane Garrett."

George nodded acknowledgement, extending a hand. "Nice to meet you, Shane Garrett."

Shane took the proffered hand. "So what exactly is the purpose of hiding out here? Do you have a plan or anything?"

George shook his head. "Right now the plan is to simply stay alive and gather as many survivors as we can until the police can get whatever's happening under control again."

Like a wet dog coming out of the water, Shane shook his body to get more loose glass shards off his clothes. "Well, from what I've seen so far, the cops are doing a pretty shitty job of it. I was supposed to meet my neighbor in the back lot but he never showed up."

George shook his head sadly. "If you're friend didn't arrive I'm afraid that probably means only one thing."

"What?" Shane asked, not understanding.

"He's probably dead, son. I mean, it's possible he's holed up somewhere, but if he didn't come and still hasn't, what other reason could there be?"

Shane looked devastated as George's words sank home.

"I'm sorry, son." George put his hand on Shane's shoulder and squeezed gently. "It seems everyone is losing people they love nowadays. Most of us still can't wrap our heads around what's happened here. It's all so unimaginable. Some say it's terrorists, biological warfare maybe. Others say it's the Rapture finally come down to Earth to punish all us sinners."

By now, most of the people that had gathered to see the new arrival had left, going back to whatever they were doing, the excitement over. George walked away, making a gesture for Shane to follow. "Leave your motorcycle, you won't be needing it anytime soon, I'm afraid. I'll have Carl take care of it for you. Everyone's returning to their posts, so why don't you come with me and we'll get you set up."

Shane glanced back at the prone motorcycle to see Carl was picking it up and then used the kickstand to keep it that way. The man began going over it to see if it was damaged in any way. Shane followed George down the wide corridor and then turned right. They walked into the small food court, and sat down at one of the thirty tables in the center of the room. Shane felt lost as he mourned Mr. McAlister, if the man was truly dead. He also pitied himself for being left alone once more.

"So, what's your story, son?" George asked as he handed Shane a can of soda.

Shane looked at him, bleary-eyed. "You really think my neighbor is dead? He could still come here."

George put on a grim smile and shook his head. "Anything's possible, son, but highly unlikely."

"Damn it! Everyone I know keeps dying. It's like I'm cursed or something," Shane said, his voice cracking.

George smiled for real now. "It's not you, Shane, it's what's happening. Everyone here in this mall has lost someone over the past few days. We all have a story."

Shane looked the man hard in the eyes. "You too?"

George nodded. "Sure, I had a family…" He trailed off and Shane could see the man wasn't going to elaborate.

The two sat quietly for a few minutes while others walked by and said hello to George, who nodded politely.

"So, can I stay here?" Shane asked. "I have nowhere else to go."

George smiled and patted the back of Shane's hand, which was resting on the table. "Of course you can, son, everyone's welcome here. But you have to pull your weight, with chores or whatever might be asked of you." George offered his right hand to Shane. "Welcome aboard, son."

Shane glanced at the hand, then shook it. He fixed his gaze on George. "So you owned a Men's store?"

"That's right. Custom tailored suits for an affordable price."

"Oh," Shane shrugged. "I think you missed your calling. You should have been a therapist, not a store owner." He meant how George had been patient with Shane and willing to listen to his concerns.

"Well, I don't think there'll be much use for either of those skills in the coming days, but I do have something else to fall back on, too."

"Which is?"

"I was a Marine a lifetime ago, and like riding a bike, it isn't something you forget."

"My dad was in the army," Shane said. "He was killed overseas."

George patted his arm. "A lot of men were I hate to say. I'm sure he was a good man. We could use some more military-trained types here right now, I'll tell you. More of those things outside are arriving by the minute and if they don't stop, I don't know how long we'll be able to stay here." He stood up. "But that's for later, for right now, let's get you some food and then find you a place to sleep." He led Shane to one of the restaurants.

Shane followed, and as they went to one of the restaurants, he thought about what George said. Maybe the man was right and

Mr. McAlister was out there somewhere, fighting the zombies and overcoming the odds.

And besides his neighbor, who knew how many other survivors might be out there?

Chapter 19

Johnson drove down the street in the jeep, swerving hard as he tried to avoid a mob of zombies. He had one hand on the steering wheel, and the other on the handle of a riot shotgun he'd found in an abandoned police cruiser.

He was searching for a gun shop, as he needed more weapons than just the riot shotgun. He made a sharp left onto a street, the name on the street sign obscured by overgrown trees. The engine made a sputtering sound, indicating it was almost out of gas. He cursed and glanced at the gas gauge. He was driving on fumes.

A gas station appeared on his right and he pulled into it, the engine dying just as he stopped at the first pump.

Climbing out of the jeep, he walked into the station, the riot gun leading the way. Broken glass littered the floor from all the windows and the door being shattered. There was congealed blood on the floor.

Johnson walked back outside, then saw the sign that there was no gas as well as no power to operate the pumps. With the jeep out of fuel, it looked like he was walking again.

As he began to head out, three zombies appeared from around the rear of the gas station. All were bloody and had multiple wounds, each one a wound that had killed them, to then have them revive as one of the walking dead.

Johnson wasn't in the mood to deal with them, and as the trio of cadavers stumbled towards him, he leveled the shotgun and fired three times.

The first blast took off a zombie's left leg at the knee, the second took off a head at the neck, and the third cut a body in half, the upper part falling to the ground, where the thing began to crawl using only its arms, intestines dragging out behind it. Johnson was already walking away, not worried about the half-corpse.

He had to admit, he was having fun. Killing people indiscriminately was a fucking blast.

Another zombie popped up from around a parked car and he shot it point blank in the chest. The zombie was thrown backwards to flop onto the sidewalk, and as Johnson reached it, he realized the man wasn't one of them at all, and that he'd shot a living person.

The man spit blood, his chest cavity a gaping chasm, and he looked up at Johnson, his eyes pleading for help. He didn't know what the man expected him to do, but Johnson knew he needed to cover his tracks like back at the farmhouse, so he lowered the muzzle of the shotgun at the man's head and fired. The head exploded like a rotten tomato, sending bone and brain matter in all directions.

As the arms and legs twitched and spasmed in death, Johnson moved on. Now no one would ever know what he'd done, the body just another corpse littering the streets of the city.

Whistling a tune, he moved on in search of that gun shop.

An hour later, Johnson came upon what he was searching for: a local gun shop.

As he opened the front door to enter the shop, jingling bells went off above his head. Freaked out, he jumped slightly and leveled the riot shotgun, thinking he was going to be attacked. Then he realized what the bells were for and felt foolish.

There were circular mirrors hung all around the shop, placed perfectly so the cashier could watch the customers in the aisles while at the front counter. The main counter had a cash register on it, the drawers open and completely empty. The ceiling was covered in white, acoustic tiles. All the aisles had been picked clean, even a mannequin that had once worn a bullet proof vest and BDUs was now naked.

Scattered on the floor were empty boxes of ammunition and a few items that were of no use to him, such as invoice forms and paperwork that needed to be filled out for a gun permit.

From the street came the sound of footsteps, scuffing the ground, and he ducked behind a cardboard cutout of a Rambo-like figure holding an assault rifle. As he hid and peered around the cardboard gun muzzle of the cutout, he watched more than a dozen zombies stumble past the shop. Mostly made up of women and children, the undead mob still looked as dangerous as any others Johnson had come across.

They never stopped and soon were past the shop. Johnson was about to come out of hiding and continue his search when one more zombie appeared, slowly stumbling down the sidewalk, following the rest of the crowd. It was a child, a toddler actually. No more than two or three years of age, the small zombie was a girl, right down to the pink overalls and a shirt with unicorns on it. Her hair was done up in a ponytail, and as she passed the gun shop, something caused her to stop and peer within the gloom of the open front door of the shop.

Johnson remained perfectly still, knowing if this zombie gave warning, the others would return to see what the toddler had found. He cursed himself for being so foolish as to leave the door open, but when he'd heard the bells he'd become distracted.

The zombie girl turned and entered the gun shop, her pale eyes flicking back and forth within her head. Johnson gripped the riot gun tighter but remained motionless as the girl walked down the center aisle.

When she was closer, he could see the large wound in the left side of her throat and see the blood staining that side of her overalls. The wound glistened in the gloom, still wet and moist. A few flies buzzed around the gaping hole, feeding on the congealing blood. He also saw she had no left arm, the limb pulled from the socket like a chicken leg from a roasted bird.

Johnson waited until the little girl was only a few feet from his hiding spot, then he jumped up and brought the butt of the gun down on her head, caving it in and sending the small body to the floor.

Then he let out a laugh at the sight. Now he was killing children. Hell, why not? All is fair in love and war, and there was no doubt in his mind that it was fucking war out there in the city right now. And who better to fight a war than a soldier?

Dark blood pooled around the little girl's head and Johnson took a step backwards, as if he was squeamish and didn't want to get any blood on his slippers—which he didn't actually.

Padding softly to the front door, he slowly closed it, careful not to let the bells ring, then peered outside to see if all was quiet.

It was.

He walked back to the body of the little girl and decided to drag it out of the center aisle, then he went back to what he'd come to the gun shop for in the first place—to search for weapons.

He walked around the rest of the shop, kicking at the empty boxes of ammunition. He went into the back but there was nothing there either. He was about to leave when he stepped on a part of the floor in the middle of the back room and heard it squeak beneath him, as well as dip slightly. Pulling back a gun-oil stained throw rug, he found a trap door. Opening it, he crept down the wooden ladder and found the secret stash of the gun shop owner.

It wasn't anything to cheer about, but there were more than enough guns and ammunition for his needs. He quickly began loading a duffel bag with ammunition and a few assorted handguns as well as taking an Ar-15 that was propped on a shelf. He only had a few more rounds for the riot shotgun and there was no extra ammo for it.

Once it was empty, it would only be good as a club. When the bag was full, he filled his pockets with loose rounds. Whoever the gun shop owner was, the man had taken the second amendment seriously. There were military BDUs there as well and Johnson changed out of his hospital scrubs and into more proper attire. There were a few pairs of boots also and he found a pair that was close to his size.

He put down the duffel bag and decided it would be best to organize the guns to fit as many as possible, so he slowly began pulling some out to reorganize, when he heard something above him, at the front of the store—jingling bells.

That could only mean one thing. The door!

Taking the bag with him, he left the hidden room and returned to the main counter at the front of the store. He'd loaded a Glock and now held it in his right hand, figuring the riot shotgun might be too unwieldy in such close quarters.

His gaze immediately went up to the mirrors. Outside, the wind had picked up and he also saw that the front door was open again. He knew it wasn't he that did that, and after the little girl, he'd made sure to close it

He slowly, cautiously walked heel to toe toward the door, checking each aisle. A low moan got his attention, and the next thing he knew, he was forced against the wall. Somehow, a zombie had managed to open the door and stumble inside. Maybe they weren't as stupid as he'd first thought.

There was movement on his left and as he turned, pale, gnarled hands were around his throat in an instant, and he gasped for air as he tried to break free, both he and the zombie falling to the floor. The Glock was knocked from his hands. He was trapped!

The face was so close to his that all he could see were the milky-white eyes, the orbs filled with hunger. The zombie's breath reeked, making Johnson want to puke and he tasted bile in his mouth as he gagged. Teeth clacked an inch from Johnson's nose as something oozed out of the corner of the zombie's mouth to splash his cheek.

He had to act fast or it was all over. He kicked out and managed to push the zombie off him a little, and the grip on his neck lessened slightly. He shoved his body forward, pushing off the floor with his back.

The zombie rolled off him some more, its teeth clacking on empty air. Johnson got to his knees, then his feet, and jumped over the zombie in a forward roll to grab the fallen Glock, then he turned around and was about to shoot but decided against it. The gunshot would attract others. Raising his right boot, he stomped the zombie's head into red mush. It took five solid blows before the skull was good and crushed.

Breathing heavily, he leaned back against a shelf and gathered himself. His heart was beating a mile a minute and he closed his mouth and breathed through his nose, slowly calming down. When he was in control and felt a little better, he went back for the duffel bag, slung the AR-15 over his shoulder after loading it, then left the gun shop, barely glancing at the body of the little girl or the one with no head. The Glock was tucked into the waistband of his pants, and the riot gun was slung over his shoulder with the AR-15.

He walked down the street and turned the corner at the next intersection, then stopped cold to see that two dozen zombies were before him. Deciding that being quiet wasn't that important over his continuing survival, he unslung the riot gun and fired the rest of the ammo into the crowd. When it was empty, he tossed it away and leveled the AR-15 at the undead mob, then began to shoot.

One by one, the zombies fell until the AR-15 clicked empty. There were still a few more zombies left but he had done what he wanted and there was no reason to take them all down. He turned and ran, the heavy duffel bag slowing him down considerably as it bounced up and down on his back, but he wasn't going to leave it. Next to food and water, what was in the bag would keep him alive.

Two blocks away he came upon a car accident, bloody and broken bodies strewn across the ground. One car, a Honda, didn't seem to have much damage to it, and he pulled out the dead driver with a broken neck and a massive dent in its head, no doubt suffering brain trauma, as brains oozed through a crack in the dent. He jumped inside the car. T

he ignition was off and he turned the key, the engine starting after the third try. Backing away from the accident, the front bumper was pulled off, as it was still jammed into the bumper of the other car. He could have cared less. He drove onward.

Chapter 20

A sign for the shopping mall came into view and Johnson took the turn for it, thinking that it would be a great place to hole up and weather the storm until the authorities got things back to normal. Checking in at the base wasn't an option and he knew he needed to worry about himself right now. If a search party found the downed helicopter, it would be assumed that he'd died in the crash and he doubted any CSI teams would be arriving to do a thorough search. Besides, the military had more important things to worry about than a rogue corporal anyway.

As he approached the mall, he saw that there were hundreds if not a thousand zombies surrounding the place. He slammed on the brakes, staring at the sight before him.

Maybe this wasn't such a good idea after all.

Then from the far right he heard gunshots, and seconds later a pickup truck came racing towards him from the far side of the mall, where the zombies weren't as thickly congregated. Three men were in the rear bed of the pickup and another man was driving. The men in the back were shooting at the closest zombies, taking them down before they could even take five steps.

Johnson sat watching until the pickup drove right up to him and the men in the rear bed jumped down. Johnson kept his hands on the steering wheel, not wanting to get a bullet from an itchy trigger finger of one of the men. The men didn't look like professionals, but rather just people thrown into an impossible situation. As the men came closer, Johnson saw that the youngest of the group couldn't have been older than nineteen or twenty. He had brown wavy hair like a rock star and a wide, cocky smile.

"Uh, hi, guys, what's up?" Johnson asked as non-threatening as possible as the men stopped and surrounded the Honda. Two stood by the front bumper and the younger man came to the driver's side window. He was smiling and that put Johnson at ease.

"Hey there, I'm Shane. Do you need a place to stay? If so, we're happy to take you in. We've set up shop in the mall. There's a bunch of us, and one more is always welcome."

Johnson looked at the pickup and the zombies approaching them. They had maybe two minutes tops before the leaders of the crowd would reach them.

Shane saw this also and nodded at the horde. "Best make up your mind quick," he said. "We can't stay here too long." While Shane was talking, the other two men were shooting at any strays coming at them from the sides, and the driver of the pickup was looking impatient to leave.

It wasn't really a difficult decision for Johnson to make. If the men had wanted to kill him, they would have already done it, and if he continued roaming around, sooner or later his luck would run out.

"I'm in, and thanks for the invitation," Johnson said.

A group of zombies came at the pickup and Honda, and the two men at the front bumper mowed them down, almost every shot a headshot.

"We need to move now, Shane," one of the men said.

"I hear you, Carl," Shane replied.

"Then get your ass in gear. All this shooting is attracting them right to us."

Shane gestured to Carl with the muzzle of his handgun. "That's Carl. He's a good guy once you get to know him. We can do the rest of the intros once we're back in the mall, though."

"Sounds good," Johnson said.

A zombie popped up right behind Shane and Johnson leveled his Glock at it. To Shane it looked like the man was about to shoot him in the face but then Johnson shifted his aim to the right slightly and fired. Shane felt the bullet zip past his ear, but when he heard the body fall behind him, he turned to see the zombie with a hole in its head.

"Shit, thanks," was all Shane could say.

"No problem," Johnson grinned cockily.

"Today, Shane!" Carl yelled as more zombies arrived. "Maybe it was a bad idea having you come out with us today!"

Shane glanced at Carl, looking hurt, but he quickly wiped his face of the look and put on a smile and faced Johnson. "Okay, so just follow us to the back of the mall. It's not as bad there and we can get into the loading dock after we lure any away from the building."

"How do you do that?"

"We park at the edge of the lot and start shooting at them. They all turn and come for us, then we skirt the crowd and zoom right into the loading dock. Though it's been getting harder as more of them show up."

"Shane!" Carl yelled one more time with anger in his voice.

"Time to go," Shane said and ran back to the pickup truck, the other two men joining him. They continued firing the entire time and even Shane shot a few that were too close. As the pickup began to drive off, Johnson followed it, staying right on its bumper.

Just like Shane said, it was simple to draw the undead crowd away from the rear of the mall, then zip by them and into the loading dock bays. More people were there to open and then close the roll-up doors as soon as the two vehicles were inside.

As Johnson got out of the Honda, Shane walked up to him again after talking quickly with Carl.

"I've been told I'm your escort 'cause I was the last arrival before you. Follow me and I'll show you the ropes, then I'll bring you to see George."

"Who's George?"

"He's kind of the leader around here. You'll like him, he's a good guy," Shane said.

He led Johnson out of the loading dock and into the main lobby of the mall. Johnson had his duffel bag with him as well as his other weapons. No one seemed to mind that he was armed. He didn't know if that was a good thing or a bad one.

Shane looked over his shoulder. "So, I never caught your name."

Johnson smiled. "I never gave it. Just call me Johnson."

Chapter 21

Shane held his hands up high, as if showing off the entire shopping mall to Johnson. "Welcome to the Seacrest Mall!" he announced, his voice echoing off the walls. People worked around them, putting items into piles or carrying objects from place to place. Even more people were making checklists of what the mall had that was of use.

Shane led Johnson down one of the long corridors in the shopping mall, pointing out this and that. "There's plenty of food for now," Shane said. "Since the power went out, all the perishables from the restaurants have been cooked on BBQ grills on the roof and when that's gone there's lots of canned food from the CVS and other food stores."

"Sounds good," Johnson said as he glanced at the storefronts. Skylights let in plenty of light in the daytime.

"George is the guy in charge around here. He's not pushy or anything; he just kind of got the job when no one else wanted it." He pointed to the heavy duffel bag Johnson was carrying. "What's in the bag?"

"Guns and ammo, a lot of it."

"No shit?"

"No shit. You seem to know how to handle a gun. Who taught you?" Johnson asked.

"My dad used to take me hunting when I was younger." Talking about his father seemed to drain Shane of energy.

"You okay?"

"Yeah, it's just…never mind."

"Where's you father now?"

"He died in the Iraq war."

"Sorry to hear that. I knew some people that died over there, too. It sucks."

"Yeah," Shane said. The two remained quiet for a few moments as they walked.

They entered a store that used to sell fine wines and cheeses. There were four people at the back counter, making Molotov cocktails with the inventory.

Shane turned to Johnson, a wide grin on his face. "You like? We're making Molotov cocktails to use against the zombies " He picked up two and handed them to Johnson. "Here, take these. You can leave your bag here, no one will touch it."

Johnson seemed to hesitate for a second, but then simply shrugged and put the duffel bag behind the counter. After all, it wasn't like he could carry the bag everywhere he went, nor could he watch it all the time. He did as Shane said and was then led to the back of the store and up a flight of cement stairs. They walked down a thin corridor to another set of stone stairs that led to a metal door leading to the roof.

It was cool out, and a gentle window was blowing the odor of unwashed and bloody bodies from the undead crowd below. In the distance, pillars of smoke could be seen from unknown fires. Sometimes if the wind was right, gunshots floated on the errant breeze as well as an explosion or two.

They walked across the roof until they reached the edge. Shane put down the Molotovs he was carrying and gazed out at the sea of zombies standing in the parking lot below.

"Jesus, will you look at them all," Johnson whispered.

"More keep coming all the time, too, that's why we need to clear out as many as we can on a daily basis. If we don't, sooner or later the shear amount of bodies will push in the glass doors on all the entrances." He reached into his pocket and pulled out a disposable lighter, leaned down, and using his body to block the wind, lit a wick on a Molotov.

Picking it up, he threw it as hard as he could off the roof. The burning bottle soared through the air, arcing downward, to land in the center of a large mass of bodies. The bottle exploded on impact and the flames spread to the closest zombies.

Fire licked up the legs and torsos of the flailing creatures. They didn't like fire and the odor of cooking flesh came to Johnson's nose almost immediately. It made him sick. Below, more of the zombies had begun to catch fire, their hair burning, their faces melting. One creature was nothing but flames, and it walked around, flailing its arms and bumping into other ones, who were soon ablaze to continue the domino effect.

A new odor permeated the air now, one of cooking human flesh, the sickly sweet odor enough to make both men gag. Johnson picked a spot in the crowd and threw one of the two bottles he held after Shane lit the wick for him. The Molotov soared out into the air and then dropped down to land directly on the head of a female zombie.

Instantly, the zombie was a wreath of flames, her eyes melting, her tongue cooking in her mouth as she opened her lips to issue a low moan. Once more, the flames spread to others and soon there was a large section of burning bodies. Many zombies steered clear of the flames, as if they sensed fire was true death. Johnson tossed his last Molotov down at the crowd and watched the bodies burn. Hundreds were in flames now, until the fire had consumed enough that they toppled to the ground.

Shane had thrown his last one, too, and both men watched the shifting sea of bodies for almost ten minutes without speaking.

The flames were dying down as the burning zombies collapsed, blackened and charred. Despite the culling, there were still far too many animated corpses surrounding the mall, and as time passed, the ones destroyed by fire became irrelevant. The fallen charred corpses were trampled on by others, pounded into the asphalt until they were ash to be spread about the area by the wind.

"That's good for now. Come on, let's go back down and I'll introduce you to George and some more people." Shane smiled. "You'll see, this place isn't so bad."

Chapter 22

Later, after Shane had introduced Johnson to George and was shown more of the mall, and Johnson had a handle on where everything was, they sat down on one of the dozens of benches that lined the corridors outside the stores and talked some more. It was while they were chatting that someone came running down the hall, yelling out to all who would listen. "There're survivors outside at the end of the parking lot. More survivors are outside!"

Everyone stopped what they were doing and ran to the roof, until more than thirty people were gathered on the edge. No one got too close, not wanting to be accidentally pushed off by someone behind them. It had almost happened once before and since then everyone was extra careful.

Across the sea of zombies, where the parking lot led to the main road and the highway, were gathered a group of fifteen people: eight men and three women and four children of various ages, though none over twelve, all a variety of ages and ethnicities.

"What are they doing? They don't really think they can get through all those things, do they?" someone said.

"They're crazy if they try, they'll never make it," another said, more people agreeing with the last person.

"Shit, they're gonna try it!" another voice cried out.

As the crowd on the roof watched, the refugees began running at the zombies, wanting to get through them and reach the shopping mall and what they hoped was salvation.

They were armed with nothing more than baseball bats, shovels and rakes, and only one or two of the men were carrying a gun. Already they were using the guns, shooting into the undead mob as they fought to get through the walking dead.

"Who are they and where did they come from?" someone asked.

"Does it matter?" another asked. "They're already dead; they just don't know it yet."

"I bet there were more of them at one point," another person added.

As the survivors fought against the tidal wave of bodies, they quickly realized they had made a tragic mistake.

"They're not going to make it," Johnson said, voicing what everyone was thinking.

"No, they can make it," Shane rebutted. "They just have to keep moving."

"No, they won't," Johnson pressed.

"They'll make it!" Shane repeated. "They have to."

"He's right, they might make it!" said a man to Shane's right.

Johnson shook his head. "They won't make it."

Seconds later, a zombie grabbed the leg of the leading man, yanking the limb out from under him and causing the man to tumble to the ground. Pulling the man back, the other zombies all dog-piled on top of him, scratching and biting. The other survivors turned around and raised their weapons, trying to retreat as more of them were taken down and torn apart. Screams and yells for mercy filled the air as the men, women and children were slaughtered one at a time. Seeing the children swallowed by the creatures was the hardest part for Shane, who finally had to close his eyes so he didn't have to look anymore.

The people gathered on the roof of the shopping mall watched in horror as the small group of survivors were killed and devoured before their eyes. Some got sick, vomiting the contents of their stomachs over the edge of the roof, where it splashed onto the upturned faces of even more walking dead.

"They didn't make it," Shane mumbled finally upon opening his eyes, his head shaking sadly. "I was so sure they would."

Johnson patted Shane on the shoulder. "Sorry, man, but they never had a chance. They were just too desperate to realize it. They must have had a few vehicles that broke down and they made a mad dash to this mall." He turned and walked away, leaving the roof, with others joining him. No one spoke, all filled with the loss of witnessing more people being killed, and all understanding that it could have been them down there.

Shane stayed after everyone else left, remaining alone, staring down at the sea of walking dead for another ten minutes, and though he fought against the wave of hopelessness filling him, he knew it was there for a reason.

Slowly, the shopping mall was changing from a place of salvation to a prison, one where the jailers were about to break in at any moment.

He continued his silent vigil, and when he'd finally had enough, he walked away from the edge to the roof access door, and went back down into the mall.

Chapter 23

A day later found Johnson on the roof of the mall, holding a bottle of whiskey, drinking from it every few seconds. Shane had been looking for Johnson to help with some chores and eventually decided to check the roof.

As Shane watched the man drink alone, he couldn't see what kind of liquor it was, as Johnson had been worrying at the label, and it was all but peeled off. When Johnson saw Shane, he patted the edge of the roof beside him, wanting Shane to join him.

Below, what seemed like a million zombies surrounded the shopping mall. If Shane had to guess, he would have figured there were a few thousand if not more. The smell of blood and offal was strong, too. The bodies were decayed, as they hadn't been dead for very long, but the other smells were still quite strong. A miasma of rot seemed to fill the parking lot below as well as a massive dark cloud of fat blowflies, which darted from body to body, feeding on whatever was exposed.

Shane went and carefully sat down next to Johnson, not wanting the soldier to think he was a wimp. Ever since Johnson had arrived, Shane had been watching him. There was something about Johnson he didn't trust. He couldn't put his finger on it, though. Gripping the edge of the roof, Shane gazed down at the pale faces looking up at him. There were all walks of life in the undead crowd, from homemakers to lawyers, to cops to mailmen to construction workers to business men to homeless people, who were probably some of the first to be killed as they were living on the streets and exposed to violence on even a normal day.

It was a regular melting pot of ethnicities as well. Spanish, Irish, Italian, black, white, Chinese and so on, all together, no one fighting, each one finally part of a common cause, which was to get at the people within the shopping mall. Who knew all it would take to unite everyone in a common goal was the dead walking?

"Want a sip?" Johnson asked, handing Shane the bottle. "It'll put hair on your balls." He decided Shane wasn't moving fast enough and he pulled the bottle back and took another sip. He drank deeply and winced as he swallowed. Johnson's face turned beet red as he let out a roar and shook his head, smiling the entire time. "Shit yeah, that'll cure what ails ya!" He handed the bottle to Shane again, practically shoving it into his chest.

Shane took the proffered bottle and looked at it, trying to discern what was inside it. Then he decided it didn't really matter. He wanted Johnson to like him so he closed his eyes and gulped down a good-sized mouthful…and instantly regretted it.

It was like a river of fire was sliding down his throat and it was all he could do not to vomit right there. The world grew dizzy and he had to hold on tighter to the roof edge or risk falling off. He began to sputter, his lips blowing out air as if he was attempting to put out a fire. His eyes began to water and he blinked back the searing pain in his gullet. It was like he'd swallowed acid! Even now he was imagining his insides dissolving and turning to mush. He may have truly believed that if he hadn't witnessed Johnson drink from the same bottle.

"Jesus…" Shane sputtered. "What the fuck is this shit?" he asked when he was able to talk again, though he waved a hand in front of his mouth to try and cool off the flames inside.

"A real man's drink, pal, that's all you need to know." He took the bottle from Shane's weak fingers and swallowed another large gulp. Smacking his lips, he let out a burp that echoed over the moans of the dead below.

"Where'd you get that?"

Johnson laughed. "In the back of the wine store. My guess is the owner wasn't a wine drinker and this was his personal stash. Funny, huh?"

"Yeah, sure, funny."

"Want some more?"

Shane shook his head as soon as Johnson asked. "Nah, I'm cool."

"Good, more for me." Johnson took a few more gulps and finished off the bottle, then pulled his arm back like he was on the mound and pitching, and he threw it as hard as he could. The bottle soared out over the undead crowd to then arc downward. It landed smack dab on the head of an undead woman with curlers in her hair. It shattered upon impact, sending the woman to her knees, where she was then crushed by the dozens of bodies surrounding her.

"Ha, one down, a fucking million more to go," Johnson slurred drunkenly.

"You're drunk," Shane said.

"Fuck yeah, I'm drunk. And if I have my way, I'll be drunker in another hour." He reached into his jacket pocket and pulled out a small bottle of Jack Daniels, then cracked it open and took a long sip.

"Why do you drink that shit?"

"Why? To forget, that's why." He pointed to the dead below. "See them?"

Shane nodded.

"Well, when you're drunk, they aren't so bad." He looked at Shane. "Shit, haven't you ever gotten drunk with your friends?"

Shane shook his head no.

"Well, man, you're missing out. I used to get wasted every Friday night with my buds before I joined the Guard." He took another long pull of the bottle, then let out another burp.

"I need to get back to the others," Shane said and got up. He was on his feet and walking away from Johnson a moment later.

"Wait, I'll come with you," Johnson said and tried to get up. But he was too drunk and his coordination was shot. As he placed his right hand down on the roof to push himself up, his hand missed completely, and before he knew what was happening, he was falling off the roof, the wind rushing through his ears.

He didn't die when he landed, as the zombies were there to cushion his fall, and thanks to being drunk, the pain of being ripped to shreds was dulled. It was over in seconds, Johnson never letting out so much as one squeak at being torn apart. The zombies began feeding on the bloody pieces, the ravenous horde finally able to taste warm flesh.

Up above on the roof, Shane reached the roof access door and turned around to see if Johnson was following him, and his eyes went wide to see that the soldier was nowhere in sight. Only the bottle of Jack Daniels was lying on the roof. Walking back to the bottle, his eyes scanned the rooftop, thinking maybe Johnson had gone behind an a/c unit to take a piss.

"Johnson, where are you?" he called.

There was no reply. Scratching his head, Shane looked down at the sea of bodies to see there was a particular large clump directly below where Shane and Johnson had been sitting, but other than that there was nothing to tell of what had happened only seconds ago.

There was a second access door at the far end of the roof, and assuming Johnson had gone and used that one, Shane let the matter drop.

He kicked the bottle of Jack Daniels off the roof and watched it soar into the air to strike a zombie on the forehead, then turned and went back inside.

Chapter 24

A week later and the situation had gone from bad to worse outside the shopping mall. There were twice as many zombies now and it was apparent to all within that the shopping mall could become a prison just as quickly as it had become the survivors' salvation.

Though many wanted to stay, the consensus was that they leave before there were so many zombies surrounding the mall that there would never be any way to escape. After all, there were a lot of people in the mall, almost fifty, and there was only so much food. Sooner or later it would run out.

George, Shane, Carl and a few other people were in the loading dock, working on a delivery truck they had acquired before things had become too difficult to leave. In the other bay was Johnson's Honda, but it was too small to be of much use as an escape vehicle.

The delivery truck was old and they wanted it in as good a shape as possible before heading back out into the world. Luckily, the mall had an auto parts store, and almost all that was needed to fix the truck was there, and what wasn't could be fashioned out of other parts, such as cutting down radiator hoses or grinding down bolts that were too long.

Carl slid out from under the truck, covered in grease after putting the bolt for the oil pan back in after draining it. Shane was right beside him, helping the man with whatever he needed, such as handing him tools.

Working on the truck reminded Shane of weekends with his father, working on his father's car, and he felt a pang of grief upon thinking of him.

"You okay?" Carl asked, seeing Shane's drawn face. He had to yell as the constant pounding of fists on the bay doors filled the loading dock with noise. It was a constant reminder that the dead were right outside, waiting.

"Yeah, I'm fine. Just thinking about my dad."

Carl merely nodded, understanding completely. He'd lost family, too, when the dead began to walk. He did his best to keep busy so as not to think about it. "I don't need you for a bit if you want to take a break!" Carl yelled over the banging.

"Okay, thanks." Standing up, Shane trudged through the bay and sat down on the center median.

John, another of the group, ran up to George who had just entered the loading dock. He stuck a notebook under George's nose. "These are some of the inventory slips you wanted, George."

"That's fine, John," George said loudly to be heard as he took the notebook, opened and glanced at it, then handed it back to John, who tucked it under one arm. George's sweaty hair stuck to his brow, his jaw taut from stress. "Please put it where the rest of them are on my desk. I'll look at them in the morning. All right?"

"No problem," John said and left the loading dock, to head to a small office at the back of the CVS that George had taken for himself.

George rubbed his temples, his eyes wishing they could close and stay that way. He hadn't slept in days, and he was mentally and physically exhausted. There was just too much work to be done, or else the entire mall could fall apart while he was sleeping. He knew he was micro-managing but he couldn't help it. He'd become the defacto leader and he took that position seriously.

He walked over to Carl, who was wiping his oil-covered hands on a rag. "How's it going?" he yelled, asking about the truck.

Carl shrugged. "Slow but steady. She's old and whoever was her owner didn't take good care of her," he called back just as loud.

"But you can fix it?"

"Sure can, just need another two days, maybe three at the worst."

George frowned. "We may not have that long, Carl!" he yelled. "Have you seen how many of those things are outside? Shit, you can hear them. We might not be able to get out of the loading dock when we open the door."

Carl didn't have a reply to that but instead said, "I need the time I need, George, and busting my balls isn't going to change that." Carl turned and got on his knees, then slid under the truck again.

Feeling snubbed but knowing there was really nothing he could do about it, George turned and walked to the office door that was for shipping and receiving when the mall was open, and stepped inside. Opening the door, he entered and upon closing the door, it thankfully became quieter.

A man in his late thirties named Mike sat behind the desk, relaxing, and he smiled as George entered. Mike's complexion was white as a ghost, as if he'd never seen the sun before. His hair was also white, and his eyes were almost completely void of color.

Mike raised a hand in greeting. "Hey, George, how's it going?"

In the last few weeks, Mike had stopped being just another nameless face and had become an asset in the mall. He was a good shot and also used his skill to teach others how to shoot. George never asked Mike why he was so pale, assuming it was some deficiency with his skin, like maybe the man was an albino, but he had to admit that the pale complexion and white hair on a man so young was off-putting sometimes.

"How's the truck coming? Will it be ready?" Mike asked.

"Carl said it should be," George replied. "Carl's a good mechanic. And the other men helping him are doing a great job."

"That's good, because I was on the roof a little while ago and it's getting worse by the hour. The noise they're making out there must be attracting even more of them from all over. We need to leave, and the sooner the better."

George nodded his head. "We will, but not before the truck's ready. It's gonna be a tight fit getting everyone into the back of that thing, too."

"Maybe not. I heard a lot of people don't want to go, maybe almost half want to stay here and wait it out."

George blinked in surprise. This was news to him. He'd heard about a few dissenters but he had no idea it was so many. "Really, I didn't know it was that many. Well, in the end, they might be the smart ones. I'm beginning to have second thoughts about leaving here."

"Why?"

"Well, for one thing, we don't know where we're going to go. We might end up out there alone, and if the truck breaks down we're screwed."

"No, George, we're screwed if we stay here. This place is gonna become a giant death trap. A few of the doors at the south entrance are beginning to buckle. We put plywood over them but now I hear the frames themselves are beginning to bend. There are simply too many of those things out there to keep them out forever. You know that. You're just scared. Shit, man, so am I. You'd have to be an idiot not to be scared."

"Still, if I'm responsible for these people and I lead them away from here only to get them killed I..." He trailed off.

"George, listen to me! We need to go now! It doesn't matter how many people come with us. We'll take as many that want to come; the rest can stay here if they want. That's all we can do."

"But we can't just leave the people that won't come! We all need to stay together. Divided we fall, it's not just a saying. These people are counting on me to save them. I can't let them down."

Mike rubbed the back of his neck and sighed. "Look, inevitably most of them won't make it anyway, especially any that are too old and sick. It's time to face facts. We'll save as many as we can. That's all we can do."

George glared at him. "So I just let the ones that want to stay alone? I say goodbye and good luck and we leave?"

"Yeah, pretty much. Even the strongest of leaders has to make sacrifices. All you can do is give these people a choice, then it's up to them to decide what they want to do. What you don't seem to get is that you're not really in charge of anything around here. We all decide our own fates in the end."

George glared at Mike for a moment, then sighed, turning his gaze to the floor. "I hate to admit it, but you have a point, though it pains me to say it. There's no way to make people believe what they don't want to believe, and I've already tried to convince them why we need to leave. You're correct, the ones that want to stay have that right. Okay, we leave as soon as Carl says the truck is ready to go."

Chapter 25

As George and Mike finished their conversation in the office, out in the loading dock, someone yelled out and gunshots were heard. Both George and Mike ran out of the office to investigate, joining Shane as he jumped up from where he was sitting and Carl as he slid out from under the truck.

In the rear of the loading dock, amongst old boxes and trash, where sunlight from the small windows on the bay doors didn't penetrate, the area was wreathed in shadows; a middle-aged man named Martin was firing into the darkness.

As the others joined Martin, the stench of death assailed their nostrils and they all had to cover their mouths with their hands. There had been the odor of death in the loading dock all the time, thanks to what seeped in through the cracks in the sides of the doors along the frames, but this was more pungent and closer.

"Whoa! Martin! Stop shooting! Stop shooting!" George yelled to be heard.

Martin turned his weary, tired eyes on George, the muscles in his hand straining as he gripped a handgun tightly. He was in desperate need of a bath, shave and a hair cut, as were many of the survivors.

"Fuck, man. There's something back there! I saw something move!"

A shadow drifted by and then disappeared and the men all took a step back.

"Yeah, I think I just saw it, too," Mike said as he pulled his .45 pistol from a quick draw holster on his hip. "Maybe one of them got inside somehow."

"Or was already here to begin with," George added. "I think when we searched the mall upon first locking this place down, someone got lazy and said the area back here was cleared when it wasn't."

"If one of those things has been in here all this time, then why hasn't it popped up before now?" Carl asked.

"Doesn't matter," Martin said. "If one of those fucks is in here, it's gonna be dead in a few seconds." He took a step forward, his gun leading the way.

The others followed Martin around a corner, and there before them was a zombie. It had fresh bullet holes in its torso from Martin's wild shooting, but otherwise it was unharmed.

"Take that bastard out!" Mike yelled as he began to fire, Martin and Carl doing the same. Shane and George weren't armed so could only watch.

The bullets stitched the zombie from crotch to neck, taking out chunks of its flesh with each hit. The zombie stood in place, but danced a jig as round after round found its bloated body.

Finally, Mike shot it in the head and it dropped to the cement floor, very dead.

As the ringing of the gunshots faded and only the pounding of fists on the bay doors could be heard, the men went closer to investigate.

The corpse's head lay at an odd angle on the floor, one eye hanging out of its socket, the other missing from the bullet Mike had fired that had put it down for good. Its arms were splayed out on either side of it, and huge chunks of meat were missing from both legs and arms. The torso was in shreds from being shot. Dark, congealed blood was splattered all over the shelves behind it, gore covering the floor. Even with all the destruction of the corpse, the mall shirt the zombie wore was clear for all to see.

Martin glared at the men and said, "See? I knew I saw something back here."

"No one said you didn't, Martin," George commented and walked over and studied the mutilated corpse. "Just like I thought. It looks like this poor fellow must have been in here when we arrived and someone didn't do a good job of searching back here." He bent down to check the body and found a small, blood-covered notebook that was in the zombie's breast pocket. He pulled it out and opened it, ignoring the blood on it and the way the pages stuck together.

After reading for a few seconds, George dropped the notebook onto the body and stood up. "I think this guy was deaf. If that's true, it explains why he never came out till now. Think about it. If he was deaf before he died, how 'bout after he returned? He never thought to leave his place back here because he never heard anything to attract his attention. Probably just sat back there and waited all this time till something made him decide to go for a stroll."

"I'm getting back to work," Carl said and walked away.

The group broke apart, everyone mumbling and talking with each other. Shane's gaze fell on Martin in particular, who was talking to people about what he'd found, how he'd saved them from being attacked.

George stepped up to Shane and patted his arm. "I wonder if there are more in this mall, maybe hiding and too stupid to come out?" He glanced at the zombie's remains and sighed. "That thing could have been real trouble for us if Martin hadn't been alert and spotted it moving around back there." He turned to face the other men still standing around. "Okay, people, the show's over, let's get back to work."

Slowly, the men did, moving about the loading dock.

Two men entered the loading dock and walked over to George and Shane. One was John and he was leading a middle-aged man with black hair and thin eyeglasses. Shane thought the man looked like his Science teacher from twelfth grade back in high school.

"Hey, George," John said. "This is Eugene. I think you'll want to talk to him."

"What can I do for you, Eugene?" George asked. "As you can see, we're pretty busy around here."

"I want to help any way I can," Eugene said. "Put me to work."

George studied the man. "Can you shoot a gun?"

The man shrugged. "No, not really. I haven't much experience with firearms. I'm a teacher, you see, not a fighter." Eugene shrugged apologetically.

George looked at Shane. "Any ideas what we can do with him?"

Shane looked Eugene up and down. "We can use him on guard duty, I guess. If he can see, he can be of help, and if there's trouble, all he has to do is tell one of the others with a gun."

"Good enough for me," George said. "You're on guard duty, Eugene."

Chapter 26

Late that night, when everyone had bedded down for the evening—with the exception of the three people on the roof on watch and the two people that roamed the mall on guard duty—the complex grew silent. Of course, that was only as silent as it could get with the zombies still banging on the glass doors of all the exits, which there were four, one for each side of the compass.

In a first floor store that sold mattresses, along with one other family, an older couple lay together on a bed, sleeping. The man's name was Paul Baxter and he was in his late seventies.

The wife's name was Mary, who was only sixty-nine. They had met forty-eight years ago at the local carnival, had fallen in love and were still married to this day. They had three children and five grandchildren, though the whereabouts of them was unknown. Mary was having a hard time with this and Paul did his best to console her.

The older couple slept in a bed in the far corner, Paul snoring like he usually did. The father of the other family in the store also snored, and the two men supplied a cadence of chopping wood that overrode the faint pounding of the zombies at the doors.

It was late, well past three in the morning, and everyone was exhausted from a full day of getting ready to leave the shopping mall. Mary was terrified to leave but Paul saw the wisdom in it. He'd served in the Navy many years ago and was a man of decision, of action. He was in good health for his age and before the dead began to walk, had gone to his doctor and received a physical and blood work.

It had all looked good, though his doctor said he should lay off the processed meats such as salami and hot dogs, at least until his blood pressure went down. He liked to exercise, walking a mile every day, and did thirty pushups a night as well as fifty crunches. He looked damn good for his age and he knew it, and once a month—sometimes twice—when Mary was in the mood, he made love to her, and knew his stamina was as good as a man half his age. Mary never complained either.

But despite all this, as Paul lay sleeping, snoring softly, he suddenly ceased snoring and his chest stopped moving. He let out a very soft death rattle, and with Mary lying on her side, facing away from him, she never knew that her husband had had an aneurism and had quietly and with no pain, passed on into the afterlife.

His bowels and bladder let go upon death, but trapped under the blankets, the odor was stifled. Seconds passed in relative silence, only the other man snoring.

Paul's eyes suddenly snapped open and slowly moved from side to side as he tried to make sense of his new existence.

Mary shifted position and sighed in her sleep and Paul turned his head to look at her. Slowly, he rolled onto his side and slid on top of her.

"No, Paul, not now, the others might here," she whispered groggily, still asleep. With the blanket now shifted, she could smell the odor of shit and urine and her eyes opened. She wondered if Paul had had an accident. It had happened once before when he had a urinary infection.

The store was all but total darkness, not even the emergency lights on now as it had been some time since the power went out. There were skylights at the front of the store and these helped to allow some moonlight to filter in to where all the beds had been set up.

In the darkness, she could see Paul over her, his head only a dim outline. Not wanting to make any noise, she placed her hands on his chest to push him off. "No, Paul, not here, we can't. I think you had an accident in your sleep. We need to get you cleaned up."

She saw only the briefest of images as Paul's head came down on her. She thought he was going to kiss her, or perhaps nuzzle her neck, and she assumed it was the latter when she felt his lips caress her throat. But then she opened her eyes even wider and let out a soft gargle when she felt utter agony on her throat directly over her carotid artery, right where she believed Paul was going to caress her. Then she felt something warm seeping under her neck and upper shoulders, and the scent of copper filled her nose, now added to the odor of shit and urine. Her mind was still trying to make sense of what was happening, when she began to hear the sounds of mastication near her ear and felt another intense spot of pain fill her neck.

She slid into unconsciousness and then death, quickly bleeding out.

No sooner did her eyes close than they were open again, this time as one of the walking dead. Paul stopped feeding and rolled off her and slowly got to his feet. She did the same. Mary didn't notice the smell of shit and urine nor did she know that this time it was from herself upon dying. Even if she did, she wouldn't have cared. She was far beyond such menial things.

She walked around the bed and joined Paul, and the two of them shuffled across the store to the next bed, where the family of three was sleeping in a full size bed.

The family's names were irrelevant, for in less than a minute, they too, would be dead when Paul and Mary fell upon them, biting and tearing at exposed flesh, feeding on warm organs torn from their prone bodies. The mother, father and little boy would revive, and with Paul and Mary, would continue on to the next store, where more survivors were slumbering.

Chapter 27

Eugene was on guard duty, his job to walk around the mall and make sure everything was all right. The thing he hated most was when he had to go to the exits to make sure the glass in the doors was holding.

When he did this, the zombies would pound even harder, stirred up at the sight of him. Many of the bodies were lying on the ground before the doors, these were the ones crushed by the pressure of all the zombies behind them. The glass on the doors was covered in blood and gore from where bodies were pressed so hard that they began to break apart.

He tried not to look at the charnel house images for too long, or else he knew he would end up vomiting. Eugene was a fourth grade teacher and his entire life had been a sheltered one. He'd never been mugged, nor bullied in the all-boys school he'd gone to as a child. He'd never worried about money, as his parents were well off and if he'd ever wanted to, he could have stopped teaching and lived off the trust his parents had set up for him. But he liked to keep busy and never wanted to be looked at as some spoiled son who never worked a day in his life.

He wasn't a fan of conflict, nor violence, and as a person who had never been put in a position where he had to fight for his life, it was easy for him to have these values.

So now, living inside the mall, with thousands of zombies outside that wanted nothing more than to tear him apart, he was finding it hard to adapt. Which was why he had volunteered to help George and the others. He'd seen many of the other survivors just sitting around and only doing stuff when they were told to. He'd decided he didn't want to be one of them; he wanted to be someone who was helping them survive. He also thought that if he was closer to George and the others who were basically running things, he would be closer to the information of what was happening than if he was just another nameless face.

A small voice inside him said he should be carrying a gun but he knew that was foolish. He'd never used a firearm and would have a better chance of shooting himself in the foot or someone else for that matter, long before he would ever have the need to use the gun in self-defense.

He stopped in the center of the mall, where a large water fountain was located. The fountain was off and the water was still. There was a large skylight overhead and the moonlight filtered down, reflecting off the coins in the fountain. Eugene found himself staring at those coins, and thinking about all the people that had tossed them there, no doubt making a wish as they did so.

Smiling to himself, he slid his hand into his right pocket and pulled out a handful of dimes, nickels and pennies. Gazing down at them, he tossed the entire handful into the fountain, then watched the ripples of the water begin and fade away. There, he figured, that was a lot of coins and each one had a wish attached.

It never hurt to hedge one's bets when things were tough, and he couldn't imagine things being tougher than they were right now.

He sat on the edge of the fountain and sighed heavily. He placed the baseball bat he'd been given next to him and stretched his arms over his head, yawning so wide his jaw cracked. He had three more hours before he was relieved and he could get some sleep.

Martin was on guard duty with him, too, but the man was somewhere on the opposite side of the mall. On the roof were three more men, but Eugene didn't know who they were.

Suddenly, what Eugene thought was a scream filled the mall and he perked up, his hand reaching for the bat. It was there and then it wasn't, and he wondered if maybe he'd imagined it. The background noise of the zombies banging on the glass doors still filled the air and it was hard to differentiate if he'd really heard that scream at all or if it had been in his head.

He stood up and took a few steps forward, his eyes trying to see within the gloom of the mall. From where he was standing at the fountain, there were four separate and wide corridors that went off to the four points of the compass. Each one led to the glass doors of an exit and the escalators that would take people to the second floor.

As he stood there, listening, nothing but the banging on the glass doors came to him. Suddenly, he heard slapping footsteps and his heart went into his throat. The footsteps grew closer and less than a minute after they first sounded, Eugene saw Martin come running towards him, the man stopping when he was only a few feet away.

"I heard someone scream," Martin said as he sucked in air. He was out of shape and the run from the far end of the mall was a hell of a workout for him. In his hand he held a pistol, though

Eugene had no idea what kind it was. Anything Eugene knew about guns was from what he saw in the movies or on television.

"Yeah, me too, but I wasn't positive," Eugene said. "It was pretty faint."

"Well, not from where I was. I heard it plain as day. Come on, we need to check it out."

"Oh, okay," Eugene said, his stomach cramping up on him at the thought of looking for danger.

Another scream sounded, this one louder and both men looked at one another.

"Are you sure of that one?" Martin asked.

"Uh-huh," was the reply.

"Come on, follow me and don't get too close to me." Martin began running down the north corridor, Eugene following.

The two men moved quickly down the wide hallway, the storefronts blurring past them. So far no one else was up, no doubt because everyone was exhausted. The entire enclave had been working non-stop to get ready to leave. The two men were in the middle of the corridor and halfway to the glass doors when they stopped running and halted in their tracks.

Before them were a half a dozen zombies, each covered in blood with mortal wounds. Martin recognized Paul and Mary and one of the other men, but the rest were faces of people he didn't know. If they hadn't been covered in blood, he may have at least recognized the faces as people he'd seen in the food court from time to time but it was all happening so fast and he wasn't thinking clearly. Just like in the loading dock, he began to panic and his first instinct was to shoot first and worry about anything else later.

Raising the pistol, he began to shoot at the approaching zombies, his finger squeezing the trigger as fast as humanly possible.

The first round hit Paul in the right shoulder, taking out a large chunk of flesh and bone. Paul's entire body flexed and bent with the impact, but other than turning slightly, he didn't go down. He righted himself and took a step forward.

Another round hit one of the zombies in the stomach, and a dark red stain began seeping into the bedclothes the zombie wore. Still, it kept coming.

One of the zombies was a child, and whether by luck or design, a round struck the small creature in the center of its face. With brain matter splattering the ones behind it, the small body dropped to the floor. The other creatures simply stepped over or walked around the fallen corpse.

Martin was screaming as loud as possible, as he fired every bullet in his clip. Almost all of the zombies went down by the time he'd emptied the pistol, but because he was firing wildly, many bullets zipped past the zombies and continued down the long corridor. Some simply went wide and struck storefronts or the potted trees that lined the corridor, but many held a straight line and only stopped upon reaching the glass doors at the end of the corridor.

The bullets struck the glass and left small holes, a few even having enough power to strike a waiting zombie on the other side of the door, but most finished their journey once they hit the glass. Where each hole appeared, small, spiderweb like cracks surrounded it. As it was safety glass, it was designed not to shatter if hit by a bullet or even a hammer, but instead it would star and fracture, to then if broken, crumble the same way automobile glass would shatter in a car accident upon impact.

The zombies at the doors never stopped pounding and each bullet hole became a small chink in the once strong armor of glass. With each fist that struck the weakened glass, more cracks appeared until the glass became opaque.

Finally, with one final blow by some unknown zombie, one of the doors shattered, the tempered glass spilling forth to spread across the floor like crystal. Another door shattered soon after and then more until the glass barrier was all but gone.

A wave of living dead bodies quickly began to pour into the openings, the first few inside tripping on the bottom frames of the doors to fall face first onto the polished tiles.

The zombies behind them stomped and trampled them into a mush of red paste, and many of them fell as well to be crushed. But soon the mob of undead humanity was remaining upright, and like shoppers rushing in for a sale on Christmas Eve, they swarmed into the shopping mall, their wails and moans filling the air and chilling each and every survivor, who upon hearing gun-shots, had awoken and were alert. Many zombies went up the escalator directly in front of the glass doors, and soon the second floor was filling up as well.

As the dead began filling the shopping mall, the odor of decay, blood and offal preceded them, and the miasma was strong enough to make even a hardened man gag.

Eugene was the first to realize what had happened, though he had no clear idea it was Martin's stray bullets that had done it. All he knew was that the glass doors had finally broken and that the survivors' sanctum had been breached.

Dropping his bat, he turned and ran. He didn't know where he was going, but he knew he wanted to get far away from that corridor.

Martin was still squeezing the trigger of his pistol as the first of the original zombies reached him and tackled him. It was Mary. She had managed to miss being hit by even one bullet fired by Martin, who was in shock and barely fought back as sharp teeth sank into his flesh. As he was ripped apart, he was still gripping the pistol, squeezing the trigger ineffectually.

Seconds later, the first of the outside zombies reached Martin and they pushed the other creatures away and began feasting, selfishly taking the body for their own.

Martin's screams were mercifully short, as was his death.

By the time the zombies were finished with him, there was nothing remaining to reanimate.

Chapter 28

When Shane heard gunshots and screams, he came awake and jumped up from the couch he was sleeping on in the back of the wine store in a small office. He didn't know what was happening but figured it had to be bad for someone to be shooting inside the mall. Quickly putting on his brand new sneakers taken from Footlocker, he raced out of the office, through the store with mostly empty shelves, and into the corridor.

A few stores down from him, at the CVS, George came out of the office he was using as his work and sleep quarters and ran through the store and into the mall proper, while Carl, and every other survivor did the same. In only a few minutes, everyone was gathered in the corridors and by the fountain, and what they saw caused many of them to fall to their knees and cry and pray.

Filling the north corridor from side to side, the bodies so closely packed there was no space on either side, was a swarm of undead corpses, all moving down the line and heading directly for the fountain and the survivors gathered there.

The second Carl arrived and saw what was going on, he began shooting with his sidearm, as did the few other survivors that had weapons.

"Forget it, forget it!" George yelled when he arrived and took in the dire situation. "There's too damn many."

"Then what do we do?" Shane yelled as he shot into the advancing undead mob with his pistol.

George shook his head as he began pushing people towards the loading dock. "There's nothing we can do, son. The mall's lost. We need to get to the loading dock and take the truck out of here."

"But it's not ready yet!" Carl yelled. "I need at least another day on it."

"Does it run?" George asked.

"Well, yes but…"

"Then it doesn't matter. If we stay here we're all dead." He began yelling at the top of his lungs. "Everyone, get to the loading dock, we're going to have to make a run for it!"

"But I don't have any of my things," a woman cried as George began pushing her. She wasn't even wearing anything on her feet, her clothing a pair of sweatpants and a t-shirt for sleeping.

"It doesn't matter. Every second counts. Everyone, run for the loading dock!" He turned to Carl who was still shooting the zombies. For every one he shot, a dozen more were there to replace it.

"Come on, Carl, it's time to go!" George yelled.

It was a tidal wave of undead humanity and it seemed like it would never stop. The moans and wails were so loud even the gunshots could barely be heard. The sound of hundreds of pairs of feet, whether barefoot or wearing expensive shoes, slapped the tiles and bounced off the walls of the mall.

Carl shot a few more zombies and then cursed under his breath. Grabbing Shane by the arm, he yelled, "Come on, kid, George is right. This place has had it."

The two men turned and began to run, soon joining other survivors who were running for their lives as well. It didn't take them long to reach the loading dock, and after making sure there was no one else coming, Carl slammed the door and locked it. The door wouldn't hold the dead back for long but it was strong enough to keep them back until they could load up the truck and make a run for it.

Women and children were standing around crying as they waited to be told where to go next and a few men looking terrified, too. Many held flashlights, which was the only illumination in the dark space. Shane tried to count how many survivors there were in the loading dock but it was too hard. As he scanned the heads, he could tell that their numbers had dwindled significantly.

"We're missing people," George said as he walked up to Shane and Carl.

Carl shrugged. "As horrible as that sounds, it's probably a good thing. The truck might not have been able to fit everyone, this solves the problem."

"But what about when we leave?" Shane asked. "I mean, before, the plan was that someone was going to toss some Molotovs off the roof in front of the bay door to clear the zombies away so we could get out. But now that's not gonna happen."

"We'll just have to make do," George said, then turned and slapped Carl on the arm to get his attention. "Okay, let's get everyone loaded up in the back. Women and children first, then the men. Carl, you'll drive and me and Shane will sit in the front with you."

Carl nodded and ran over to the truck where he opened the rear door and began yelling out to gather everyone around. He quickly gave instructions and the loading began. The truck was the size of a mid-size U-haul moving van and a compact car would have had just enough room to be driven inside it.

"Shane," George said, "have you seen Johnson?"

Shane shook his head. "No, not for a day at least, but I figured I was always missing him. You know, this place is pretty big."

"I guess he didn't make it," George said sadly. "What about Mike, Martin, Myra or Eugene?"

Shane shook his head.

"Well, if they're still in the mall, they're on their own now, God help them. If so, I wish them luck."

While the loading of survivors commenced, the loading dock door leading into the mall began to shudder on its frame, as the zombies arrived and began to pummel it. George's eyes went to the door as he leveled a flashlight beam on it and he swallowed the knot in his throat. The frame was already cracking and it was only a matter of time before the door gave out. He considered trying to barricade it but decided there was no point. They would be loaded into the truck in a few minutes and then what happened, happened.

Turning, he grabbed Shane by the arm, and the two of them dashed to the truck to help with the loading of personnel.

Chapter 29

The last survivor was put into the back of the truck by the light of flashlights when the loading dock door leading to the mall finally gave in and collapsed. The door had been made of a veneer of metal, but beneath that it was of wood, and though it looked strong, it was just a facade, one the zombies took full advantage of.

As the door crashed to the floor, and the first bodies began to pour into the loading dock, Carl swung around and began shooting at them.

He dropped three in as many seconds but there were far too many to ever halt the tide, so he turned and ran for the cab of the truck, jumped up into the already-open door, and climbed in just as the lead zombie reached the back of the vehicle. Slamming the driver's door, he swung his head to the right where Shane and George were already waiting.

Shane was at the passenger window and he was hanging out it, shooting zombies with a calm he'd never thought he could have. His father's voice was in his head, telling him this was the time he needed to be brave. This was a moment that defined men, and separated the cowards from the heroes.

"I'll open the bay door," Shane said and prepared to jump out of the cab and make a run for the hanging chains that were set up in a loop near the right-side of the door. Pulling the chain would roll the door up. It had an electrical switch as well, but without power, manually was the only way to get the door up.

"No, Shane," Carl said, "Don't go over there!"

"Why not? If we don't get the door open, this is gonna be a pretty short trip."

"Yeah, but as soon as you pull on that chain, this bay will be filled with zombies. You won't make it back to the truck fast enough."

"Sure I will," Shane rebutted.

"No, you won't," Carl snapped.

"Then how are we gonna get outta here?" Shane asked. A zombie came up to his side of the truck and slapped the door and he jumped in his seat, but he fought to keep his face neutral.

"You're planning on running the door, aren't you?" George asked.

Carl nodded. "There's no other choice." He started the engine and it came to life on the first try, the headlights also coming on to reflect light off the metal door. Black smoke belched out of the exhaust and it quickly began to fill the loading dock. A few zombies were standing directly behind the exhaust and they were instantly covered in soot, one getting hit right in the face. It didn't care, even when its eyes became so covered with soot it was blind.

Carl revved the engine and put the transmission into first gear. It was a standard and the clutch grinded and groaned like a living beast. Carl winced. He hadn't had time to get to the transmission and fix it yet, and he knew it was on its last legs the first time he'd sat in the driver's seat and gone through the gears.

"Okay, here goes nothing," Carl said and floored the gas pedal as he prepared to release the clutch. More black smoke belched out of the exhaust. Then, like a beast finally set free of its cage, the clutch was released and the truck surged forward, directly at the closed bay door.

Chapter 30

As the truck lunged forward, the zombies surrounding it were thrown off of it, one falling directly below the front right tire. The truck rolled over the corpse, the pressure causing the upper half to literally explode outward, as if the body had been a flesh-tube of toothpaste rolled up from the bottom until the cap exploded. Only it wasn't toothpaste that shot out of the jagged neck stump as the head popped off, it was the insides of the zombie, the organs spewing out of the hole to splash onto the concrete.

The engine roared loudly as Carl revved it so that the needle on the dashboard was in the red, and when the front bumper hit the loading dock door, all the power of the eight cylinder engine was behind it.

If the door had been made of wood or fiberglass, no doubt the truck would have broken through easily, but the door was made of metal, and was flexible so it could roll up, like an accordion. So when the truck hit it, the door didn't so much as break as it did bend, and as the vehicle moved forward, it simply ripped the door out of its frame, causing it to fall forward, slapping down heavily onto the crowd of zombies closest to the building.

As the door landed heavily, bodies were flattened, others just knocked down. But the truck was still moving, and as the two front tires slipped and squealed on the slippery metal, the rear-wheel drive pushed it forward, until the truck was driving over the metal door.

The sound of crunching, squashing, squishing and pulverizing came to the ears of the three men within the cab as the truck's weight pressed the metal door down to the ground, turning the bodies beneath it into a red paste of gore and congealed blood. With the zombies being dead, the blood within their veins was all but irrelevant.

When the truck was all the way on the metal door, the full weight of the vehicle and all its passengers came full down on the zombies beneath the door. Like a piece of plywood flattening a birthday cake, gore squirted out on all four sides to splash the undead crowd still standing there.

But though more than sixty bodies were crushed under the door, there were still thousands in the parking lot, and they quickly swarmed over the truck as Carl fought to keep moving. Thousands of bodies, all packed tightly together, meant that the truck could get no momentum, and as it rolled off the door, the vehicle was already beginning to slow down.

Pressing the gas pedal to the floor after shifting into second gear, Carl gritted his teeth as he fought for another inch of traction.

"Come on, Carl, go," George said. "Get us the hell out of here!"

"What the fuck do you think I'm trying to do?" he yelled back. "There's too damn many of them, I can't get any traction. Jesus, they're all around us."

From above, if anyone had been looking down, they would have seen a sea of bodies, and in the middle, one small isolated island, which was the roof of the truck.

As more and more zombies tried to get at the vehicle, it began to rock back and forth, the shocks squeaking loudly. Carl put the transmission into reverse, backed up a few feet, and knocked bodies down, then put it into first again, flooring the gas pedal once more.

As the truck surged forward the few feet that Carl had managed to clear for himself upon backing up, a massively large fat woman stepped into the truck's path. The fat woman was naked with rolls of flesh and had to weigh four hundred pounds easy. She'd been dead since the beginning and her flesh was covered in blotches and had cracked in many places. In fact, she was so fat that the folds of flesh seemed to hang from her face, neck and arms, as if she were made of soft dough. Half her hair was missing, having fallen out from decay.

As she walked forward, everything quivered like jello, but what was odd were her fingers were small and dainty, with bright red nail polish. Her pendulous breasts were flabby, the size of large dinner plates, the nipples as big as tea saucers, with thin black hairs surrounding the areolas. A chubby chaser would have been in Heaven, but the three men inside the cab liked their women with a little less meat on their bones, so all three were disgusted at the sight of the rotting behemoth before them.

Carl never slowed down when the fat woman stepped into the truck's path, and he hit her going over thirty miles an hour. The entire truck shook with the impact, the body exploding like a popped balloon, due to the internal decomposing gases that had been growing over the past few days. To the three men inside the cab, it was like someone was standing before the truck with a giant bucketful of gore. Blood, pus and internal organs splashed the front of the vehicle, the grille and the windshield becoming covered in a miasma of putrefaction.

The smell was incredible as it cooked on the engine and George couldn't take it. He leaned forward and vomited all over his shoes and the floorboard.

Not able to see through the windshield, Carl had to turn on the wiper blades to clear the glass. Pus and blood slid off to pool on the hood.

"Jesus Christ," Shane said, amazed. "I wouldn't have believed that if I hadn't seen it with my own eyes."

"God, that was horrible," George said as he wiped his mouth with the back of his arm. "So much blood. She was so…fat."

The engine was making an odd sound and Carl fought through the gears, trying anything to keep them moving. Bodies were everywhere, pressed tight against the truck, some becoming jammed in the tire wells. As the truck moved a few inches, the bodies were wrapped around the tires like plastic bags when a car drives over one in the street. The bodies were ground into a fleshy paste beneath the churning tires. The odor of rotting flesh was so strong that all three men had to breathe through their mouths or risk continually vomiting.

The tires weren't even on the ground anymore, as they now rolled over nothing but flesh and bone. A carpet of rotting bodies was beneath the truck, and the rear tires began to slip and slide, as if they were stuck in mud. The engine was redlining as Carl fought to keep the vehicle moving, but he could already see it was hopeless. There were simply too many zombies to get through. The odds were against them, but he refused to stop. Shifting into another gear, he floored the gas pedal yet again, the engine roaring as it fought to keep the truck moving.

Chapter 31

In the back of the truck, in the cargo area, the thirty-plus survivors screamed and cried, not knowing what was going on. As the truck surged forward and back as Carl tried to get through the sea of bodies, they tried to hold on, though they were constantly knocked to the floor again and again. Only a few flashlight beams broke the darkness and each survivor let their imaginations go wild as they thought what was happening on the other side of the truck walls.

Carl, Shane and George knew exactly what was happening…and it wasn't good.

As if the bodies were nothing but six feet of packed snow, the truck worked its way through them, crushing and flattening one after another, but no matter how much Carl worked the engine and gears, he barely made it ten feet.

Shane was at the passenger window, shooting at every zombie that came up to the truck, but there were always a hundred more to take the place of the one he shot. George sat in the middle, holding spare clips when Shane ran out. He wanted to shoot too but there was only room for one person at a time at the window.

The truck's engine began to falter and both Shane and George turned their heads to look at Carl, who shook his head, not understanding why the engine was failing. "I don't know what's wrong, damn it!"

And he never would. The only way to find out would have been to get out of the cab and go to the engine and inspect it.

Unknown to Carl, so many bodies had been run over that they were becoming jammed beneath the undercarriage and body parts were being pushed up into the engine compartment. Like it was being packed with ice, bloody parts surrounded the engine on all sides, cooking and searing to the exhaust and manifold. But that wasn't what was causing the engine to stall, that was due to a torso that had been jammed up into the fan blade, and with the blade unable to turn, the linkage connecting it to the engine also stopped moving. Then, something within the engine failed and the engine began to stall.

Carl tried to work the gears but there was nothing he could do and the engine finally sputtered one last time and seized. He tried to restart the engine but all it did was make a tearing, metal-like grinding sound, one so loud it filled the cab and drowned out the noise the walking dead were making.

"What the fuck are you doing, Carl?" George yelled. "Get this thing going?"

Carl spun on George, his own panic threatening to overwhelm him. "I told you this truck wasn't ready yet! I said I had to do more work on it!"

"I don't give a shit about any of that!" George snapped back, panic filling him as well, his face beet red. "If you don't get us moving again, we're all dead!"

With the truck not moving, zombies were now climbing on the front and sides of the vehicle. They began slapping the windshield. Only Shane's side wasn't too bad as he continued shooting at any that tried to get on the vehicle. Concentrating on shooting, he wasn't even aware that the truck wasn't moving.

"Get the fuck out of the way!" George yelled. "I'll drive." He began shoving Carl, all sense of composure lost on him. He'd never been a weak man, but being surrounded by a sea of walking dead was enough to make even the toughest man crack. George didn't want to die here, he wanted to live and escape the zombies and as far as he was concerned, this fucktard Carl was preventing that from happening.

"No, George, I'm telling you that it's dead! The engine won't start. Stop it!" Carl yelled. There was really no reason for Carl to care if George wanted to try the ignition a few times but he had been responsible for driving and fixing the truck and he now took it personally that George didn't believe him when he said the engine was broken. Foolish, perhaps, but men and their egos had been the downfall of many a nation.

"And I said I don't care, I want to try! Now get the fuck out of the way...or else," George said again, his voice taking on a sinister quality.

"Or else what?" Carl prompted as his hand reached down for his sidearm.

But George was slightly faster and he raised his handgun and aimed it at Carl. "Or so help me I'll kill you and toss you out to be eaten by those things."

Shane, still shooting, had no idea of the standoff happening only two feet behind him. He was concentrating on only shooting the zombies in the head and so was maximizing his ammunition.

The two men locked gazes, both needing an outlet for the fear they felt but didn't want to accept as being part of their psyche. In normal circumstances, what was happening never would have even begun, as George was a rational man who beloved in talking over violence. Carl wasn't as mild-mannered, but he never felt the need to flex his manhood in other people's faces. He was content with who he was and was happy to defer to another male if it benefited his needs.

But inside the cab of the truck, with tension high and both men at the point of breaking, an outlet was needed, and it was easier to square off against another single, human being than thousands of animated corpses.

Carl pulled his gun but George had already had his slightly raised and both men leveled them at the same time and fired.

Though both sat only fifteen inches from one another, the rocking cab caused their bullets to go wild and neither man was shot in the head, which was where both men had aimed their guns. George was shot in the upper left shoulder and he screamed as the bullet went in and then out again to strike the windshield and crack it. Carl let out a soft grunt as the bullet meant for the center of his skull only grazed his temple to then hit the driver's side window and shatter it.

Outside, the noise of the gunshots incensed the zombies and they began to rock the truck even more. Back and forth on its shocks it shook until it began to threaten to tip over.

Shane spun around at the sound of gunshots and saw that both men were holding their guns but weren't aiming them out any window to shoot the zombies. Then he saw that George was bleeding and he tried to figure out what was going on. Shane was smashed against the dashboard as the cab rolled back and forth like a ship on rough seas. "Jesus Christ, they're gonna flip the truck!" he yelled as he held on for dear life.

No sooner did Shane announce this than the truck went to the far left and the tires on the right side went up in the air. It may have dropped back down, but as soon as the tires were in the air, zombies swarmed in beneath them, and thus prevented the precarious balancing act from returning to normal. With more bodies pushing on the tires, the truck finally gave up its balancing act and toppled over.

Though it fell over hard, the truck rolling could have been much worse if it wasn't for the fact that the sea of bodies on the side of the truck became a cushion so that the truck landed easily on its side, but the passengers inside the rear compartment and cab were still thrown about as if they were toy dolls in a barrel rolling down a steep hill.

Like a wounded animal lying on its side, the tires of the truck still spun slowly from the hands that had been pushing on them moments ago.

And much like a wounded animal, now helpless, the zombies attacked the downed truck in full force.

Chapter 32

When the truck rolled over, the passengers in the back cargo area all yelled and screamed for help, not understanding what was going on.

As the truck fell onto its side, many survivors were crushed to death under the weight of their fellow passengers as everyone fell onto each other.

The rear door wasn't locked from the outside and a man who had managed to make it through the capsizing unhurt, crawled over fallen bodies, grabbed the latch seen by the light of a fallen flashlight, and opened the door, thinking that escape was the only option.

As moonlight spilled into the interior of the truck, the man quickly realized his mistake, and that he'd doomed them all to a horrific death.

Dozens upon dozens of zombies poured into the truck, biting, clawing and tearing apart the trapped survivors of the shopping mall. A father, who had managed to hold onto his seven-year-old son, wrapped his left hand around his son's neck and the other around his chin, then he twisted as hard as he could. Tears were in his eyes as he snapped his son's neck, and thus saved his boy from being eaten alive.

A few survivors, figuring out that the door opening was their doom, still did their best to fight back. One man, a burly fellow topping six feet, with fists like hams, punched and brought down more than a score of zombies before he was finally overwhelmed and taken to the ground to be torn into bloody ribbons.

None escaped the onslaught and the victory of the dead was all but complete as the neck of one of the last remaining survivor's was torn open and the creatures fed on the spraying blood.

Many of the survivors had enough of their bodies left to re-animate, and they too, turned on any humans still not killed, though they were few and far between.

The last survivor was a one-year-old child, that sat in the back of the truck, its mother's body covering it in the hopes of saving the child. The mother was dead from a broken neck when the truck overturned, but she had cradled her child and protected it from being hurt.

Four zombies found it soon enough and picked it up at the same time, two grabbed a leg each and the other two an arm each. A tug of war began as the child cried and screamed for its mother, the pain of its stretching limbs unbearable.

When the shrieks of pain seemed like the child could yell no more, the first limb let go with ripping flesh and tendons. and a small spatter of blood squirted out of the jagged hole where the limb once was.

The other zombies, seeing the blood, yanked harder and each limb was yanked clean from the body until one zombie was lucky enough to have the arm it was holding and the torso and head connected to it. Turning and moving against the wall of the truck, it began to feed on the torso, its teeth tearing into the soft, pink flesh. The others were content to feed on the limbs they had procured, gnawing on the small, severed limbs as if they were chicken legs.

The inside of the truck was a charnel house, the side of the truck, which was now the floor, covered in inches of blood and gore, the survivors now swallowed whole by the undead horde.

The zombies that managed to fit inside the truck ate well this night.

Chapter 33

Carl was dead; his gun had gone off and he'd accidentally shot himself in the chest as the truck overturned. George was the first to move.

Shane was unconscious next to him after whacking his head on the windshield when the truck rolled over. There was a small red spot on the inside of the glass where he'd struck it with his forehead.

Panicking, George climbed over Shane's still form to the open passenger window, which now was looking up at the dark sky. It was every man for himself, as far as he was concerned, and there was no way in hell he was going to stay inside the cab of the truck.

Zombies were pounding on the windshield, and with the bullet hole in the glass to get it started, it would be less than a minute before the glass shattered and anyone remaining inside the cab would have a very bad night.

Using Shane's unconscious body as a step stool, George pushed himself up until he was able to wrap his hands around the edges of the window frame, then he pulled himself up, straining the entire time. It was like doing chin-ups and he was out of shape. But he forced himself to keep going, and as the first shards of glass

from the windshield began to fall into the truck cab, he was climbing out of the vehicle and onto the door.

It was as he was sliding his body out onto the door, that the
truck shifted from all the bodies pushing on it. George lost his grip
and slid right off the truck and into the crowd of zombies only a
few feet away. His eyes were wide, his mouth open in a silent
scream as he felt himself falling for the briefest of moments. Then
he was landing on top of bodies and was smashed to the ground,
where dozens of legs and feet surrounded him.

Rolling onto his stomach, he began to crawl through the legs.
The zombies, so closely packed together, couldn't reach down and
grab him and with so many side by side, they couldn't hold him.
A few did try though and he barreled through their legs, shrug-
ging off their grips as he trundled across the parking lot.

He kept moving for almost ten minutes and he was very positive that he was going to make it to the end of the zombies, but as
time passed and he kept moving, he began to wonder if there was
even an end to this sea of undead flesh.

The odor of decaying meat from the rotting corpses suffused
his nostrils, causing him to vomit multiple times, until his throat
was so raw he could barely speak if he'd needed to. His hands and
knees were covered with blood and pus from the gore dripping
from the bodies to splash onto the ground. One time he slipped
and he went face first into a puddle of gore, tasting it as his mouth
had been open. Spitting out maggots and bile, he vomited yet
again and relished the taste of his stomach acid over the gore.

An hour later, his arms and legs throbbing in agony from the
strain of crawling, the palms of his hands and his knees bloody
from scraping against the asphalt, he started to lose hope.

Another half hour later and exhausted, he was all but resigned
to giving up and dying. How could this be? How could he have

been crawling for almost two hours and still not reach the end to the crowd?

What he didn't realize is that his sense of direction was skewed and he'd been going around in circles. He would never reach the end of the massive crowd, not without standing up and looking to see where he was and where he needed to go. But to do that would have been certain death so all he could do was keep crawling.

Another hour passed and George's limbs were now shaking. It was getting harder to fend off the zombies, too. His vision was blurry and he had a headache and it was torture to put one hand in front of the other.

And then, as he pushed through a forest of legs, he came face to face with a zombie with no lower torso. It blocked his path, holding itself up with its hands, the body sliced in half at the stomach. Intestines hung out of the bottom of it and trailed behind it like a dozen plump strings. Perhaps it had been in a car accident, George's mind fleetingly thought, not that it mattered.

George and the half-zombie stared at one another for almost ten full seconds, as above him zombies shifted and moved, trying to reach the shopping mall and the truck.

At first George's face was neutral, and as he stared at the thing before him, he was able to see past it, and amidst the shifting legs, he spotted the undercarriage of the truck. After all this time, he'd been going in circles. He was right where he'd started. Though it spelled his death, he found this funny, hysterical actually. He began to laugh, long and loud. He pushed up on his arms and sat down on his butt, his legs throbbing with finally getting to rest. George laughed harder as the half-zombie moved one arm, then another to get closer to him.

By now, George was laughing so hard that tears were in his eyes, and as the zombie reached him and sank its teeth into his face, he was laughing so hard he was practically screaming

The zombies surrounding George quickly realized there was fresh meat below them and they stopped shuffling and bent over, grabbing George and sinking teeth and nails into his flesh.

George never stopped laughing as they tore him apart, and no matter how much pain he was in, he found he couldn't scream, laughter being the only way to deal with his impending death.

He laughed for a long time.

Chapter 34

Just as George pushed off Shane and scurried through the open passenger window, Shane came around, blinking as he tried to figure out where he was and what had happened. Something was poking him in the back, too. His hands began searching for his pistol and he found it a few seconds later.

It had been trapped under his body, and now that he'd taken it out from there, the object that had been poking him in the back was gone.

Moonlight came into the window above him but that was it. It was loud around him, and with his head hurting, it felt like a locomotive was in his head, one that was doing circles on a track.

Something soft was beneath him and he opened his eyes wider and realized it was Carl. George was gone and Shane was too disoriented to give that any thought. The truck shifted a little and he heard screams—human screams—coming from behind him, exactly where the rear cargo compartment was.

Once more, he didn't give it too much thought. He was dazed from his blow to the head and he was trying to make the world stop spinning. Turning so he was face to face with Carl, he tried to wake the man up when he saw that Carl wasn't moving, his eyes closed.

"Hey, Carl, wake up, man, we need to get out of here," Shane whispered, not sure if Carl could even hear him.

Blood drops were appearing on Carl's cheek and Shane reached up to see that it was coming from his own forehead. When he pulled his hand away, his fingers were covered in red.

"Shit," he muttered and returned his attention back to Carl, who now seemed to be awake. Well, his eyes were open. But as Carl began to move his head slightly, the moonlight caught his eyes and Shane saw that his irises were void of color.

"Shit," Shane said again, knowing what that meant. Carl began to try and right himself, his arms reaching out to wrap Shane in their embrace, but he wasn't having any of it. The two men began to fight in the confines of the cab, while only a few feet away, the windshield began to crack as countless fists pounded on it.

"Carl, cut it out, it's me, Shane!" he yelled, as if he could reason with an undead Carl. The reply from Carl was a low moan and teeth that clacked on empty air.

Shane slipped and fell hard onto Carl and then let out a scream when Carl sank his teeth into his right ear. Shane punched Carl in the face but the teeth remained where they were.

Using the pistol as a bludgeon, Shane brought it up and then down as hard as he could, and four blows later, Carl finally let go.

Carl was trapped slightly under the steering wheel and Shane pushed himself off the man. As he tried to suck in air, the windshield on his right finally shattered and hands began reaching in for him, some scratching his arms while others snagged his shirt and pulled on it. Shane began shooting them, each round right in the face, and the bodies slumped in the opening, which slowed the others behind the vanquished ones.

Shane felt another hand grab him from within the cab and he looked down to see Carl was still active, and was pulling himself out from beneath the steering wheel.

Shane leveled the gun and shot Carl in the face, right through the right eye. Skull and brain matter blew out the back of Carl's head to splatter the driver's side door red.

Shane turned and focused on the zombies before him. A sound from above had him glancing up, and where there was once night sky through the open passenger window, now there were three zombies. One slipped forward and fell onto Shane, who found himself smothered by rot and decay as the creature tried to reorient itself to bite him.

Shane punched it in the face and then grabbed its head between his hands; this was awkward, as he still held the gun. He used his left forearm to push the pale and bloody face away from him, then he brought the gun around and jammed the muzzle into its mouth. Without hesitation, he squeezed the trigger, blowing out the back of the creature's lower skull and severing its spine. It collapsed on top of him like a sack of flour.

He shoved it off him so that it was propped up on the dashboard as more zombies pulled out their dead brethren to take their chances inside the cab.

Shane had a half second to pop the clip on the pistol and he saw that he only had three more rounds left. Where more clips were was anyone's guess and he wondered if the bag with extra clips was under Carl's corpse. If it was, it might as well be a million miles away for all the good it would do him.

A zombie lunged through the shattered windshield, its body so decomposed after more than week in the sun so that Shane couldn't tell if it was male or female. He panicked and shot it in the face, the body slumping down. Its face landed right in his crotch and Shane pushed it away with a yelp, not wanting to think of what could have happened if it hadn't been dead.

Two bullets left and nowhere to go.

He pushed himself back against the seat as far as he could go and punched and kicked anything that came at him. Using the pistol as a club, the butt of the gun was soon covered in blood, hair and gore.

But for every zombie he stopped, a hundred more were right behind it. The walking dead began pulling more of the still bodies out of the windshield and Shane knew with the barricade of corpses gone, more would swarm in.

Another zombie moaned from above him and he looked up in time to see a female zombie sliding through the open window. He raised the gun and shot her as she fell on him. The bullet went right into her open mouth and out the back of her head. She landed on Shane, dead, and he screamed and pushed her to the side, where she fell onto Carl in a position that made the two dead bodies look as if they were making out.

One bullet left.

As he stared at the faces of death before him, hands reaching out to tear him apart, blood pooling inside his collar from his torn ear, he accepted that there was no hope of escape, that his life was now measured in seconds.

He thought back to a day with his father when he was only ten.

They had been fishing on a lake a few miles from their house. The boat was small, only the two of them having enough room plus their fishing gear, and his father had a cooler of beers with him and a few sandwiches for when they got hungry. Though only eleven, his father cracked open a fresh beer and handed it to Shane. "Want a sip, son?"

"Really, Dad?" Shane asked, amazed that his father was going to let him have a sip of beer.

"Sure, son, it's just us men out here after all, right?"

"Sure, Dad, just us men." Shane had taken the beer and had taken a deep pull from the can. The taste was like anything he'd ever tasted before and the bubbles had tickled his tongue. He went to drink some more but his father had taken the can back.

"That's enough of that for now, Shane," his father had joked. "I don't want to bring you home drunk. Your mother would kill me."

Shane had nodded, his stomach feeling weird as the beer hit it.

They'd fished silently for a few minutes and then Shane asked, "Dad, what's Heaven like?"

His father had given his reply after a moment's thought and Shane didn't know at the time that his father wanted to give a good answer, and not just say anything to shut his son up, who liked to ask lots of question about almost everything.

"Well, Shane, different people have different opinions on what that means, but if you want to know what I think Heaven is, just me mind you, I think Heaven is anyplace you want it to be. If it's a place you love than it's Heaven."

"So then us fishing is Heaven?" Shane asked.

His father smiled at him and rubbed his hair. "Yes, Shane, to me this is Heaven. Just you and me alone, together, a father and son, spending time together. These are the memories I keep with me when I'm on tour in another country. When I'm in those places that are like Hell, I keep these memories with me and so I take a small piece of Heaven with me." He saw Shane staring at him with wide eyes and said, "Does that make any sense to you?"

"Sorta."

"Well, maybe when you're older you'll understand better what I'm trying to tell you."

Before Shane could answer, he'd gotten a bite on his fishing rod and the two had had to deal with that.

Shane had caught a ten pound trout that day and now, trapped inside the cab of the truck, he thought back to that day and decided that yes, he now understood what his father had been talking about, and that being with his dad, on that boat, fishing, had been a slice of Heaven, and he now pulled that memory to him, wrapped himself with it, as Hell surrounded him on all sides.

Shane heard his father's voice in the back of his head say, "It's okay, son, you did your best. It's time to go. I'm proud of you, son. I'm waiting for you, come join me…the fishing's great up here."

As the zombies pushed and shoved their way into the cab with Shane, and began to wrap their arms around him and sink their teeth into his exposed flesh, he placed the warm muzzle of the pistol into his mouth and squeezed the trigger. But as the bullet blew out the back of his skull, it didn't matter anymore.

He was already gone.

He'd found that small piece of Heaven in his head with his father, and nothing else mattered.

Epilogue

It had been more than five days since the dead had broken into the shopping mall and Eugene had run for his life.

He'd found a storage room at the back of a Spencer's novelty store. With him in the storage room was stock for the store. Pretty much everything in the storage room was useless for his survival. Spencers was a gag gift store and whatever the theme of the month might have been.

If you wanted a six inch farting Santa that pulled down its pants, action figures of the latest horror craze, piercings for your nipples or dick, or perhaps some rated R sex toys and lotions, Spencers was the place to go. But if you were starving and hadn't had anything to drink in days, Spencers might not be the best choice to hole up in during a zombie apocalypse.

Eugene knew he didn't have many more days left, that he was dying of starvation and dehydration, and there was absolutely nothing he could do about it.

He'd considered drinking his own urine from where he'd peed into a small bowl that was supposed to be for Halloween candy, but in the end he'd decided against it. What would be the point? It would only prolong the inevitable anyway.

There was a constant pounding on the door, the undead having filled the store and the rest of the shopping mall. Packed shoulder to shoulder, the zombies were as trapped within the building as he was, only they didn't seem to understand their fate.

He did.

Another day passed and he could barely lift his head. Despite the constant pounding, he spent all his time sleeping, and defecating or urinating wasn't an option anymore, as there was nothing inside him to come out.

Though never a man of courage, it was then and there that Eugene decided if he was going to die, he would at last pick his time and not let fate tell him when he was going to go.

One thing he did find in the storage room that was of use were novelty birthday candles, and with novelty cigarette lighters, he at least had light to see by.

Using what little energy he had left, so weak that he wasn't able to stand, he searched the bottom shelves for something sharp, that he could use as a blade.

He searched for hours, having to take many breaks to rest, sometimes napping, but each time he woke up, he would begin the search anew.

And then he found it, a small letter opener, the plastic handle molded into the shape of Homer Simpson's face. Though a gag gift, the tip was sharp, and with the last of his strength, he used it to open his arm and wrist from top to bottom, then he switched hands and though struggling now, opened the other as well, both cuts vertically along his arms. What blood came forth was barely a sputter.

He dropped the letter opener from limp fingers, Homer's face smiling up at him as he closed his eyes. Back when the dead began to walk, he'd heard the news say that cadavers were reanimating, but as a teacher, a man of science, he found that hard to believe. Someone was paying off the news to lie. He assumed it was all from a botched government experiment and now it had to be covered up.

Still, if what the news said was true, then when he died, he would return and perhaps, just maybe, his intelligence would remain, and on top of that, maybe even his soul.

These were the thoughts that went through his head as he let out one last breath, his death rattle filling the storage room, lost amongst the pounding of the zombies.

Days, perhaps weeks later, the lock on the storage room door finally gave in under the onslaught of pounding fists and it slammed opened and to the side, the lock shattered, splintered wood from the frame raining down on the floor.

The first zombies in line prepared to rush in, to feed on the human they knew was within, but as the door crashed in, they stopped cold and then slowly moved backwards.

Out of the storage room Eugene shuffled, his complexion bone white, his eyes void of color.

As he moved his body, the wounds in his arms flexed and opened, like long, thin mouths.

Without acknowledging the other zombies, he began to push himself out into the mall, shoving his brethren aside as he began his search for human flesh.

ZOMBIE TALES

Edited by Vincenzo Bilof

The earth cannot contain the dead, graves opening wide to disgorge rotting bodies!

Maggot-filled, bloated with dripping pus, these mindless creatures only have one need—to feed on human flesh!

The zombie lives again in this anthology, filled with hungry corpses that can't get enough. Death, despair and loss, all will be experienced as you are taken on a trip into the very bowels of Hell.

The living dead are not forgiving, nor do they feel pity.

As you feel their cold embrace, and their teeth sinking into your throat to tear out your jugular, just pray it's a quick death, before oblivion claims you.

DEADLY HUNT
by Mariah Deitrick

When extreme hunt enthusiast, Drake Marshal, began his career as a hired hunter, he had no idea he would one day become the prey. If he had, he never would have found himself running for his life in a zombie-infested jungle.

Will Drake's years of hunting experience be enough to keep him alive? Or will he let his sympathy for others get him killed.

CAVALCADE OF TERROR
A HORROR ANTHOLOGY

Edited by Vincenzo Bilof

Ghosts, monsters and serial killers abound in this collection of horror stories not for the faint of heart, written by both established and up and coming new authors.

In the darkness within us all resides a demon no one can destroy, one that feeds on carnage and mayhem. Though you may try to deny this, you know it's true. Human beings are no more than animals, filled with selfishness, greed and evil intentions.

Will you face your true self or continue hiding in the shadows?

If unsure, then delve into these pages of terror and unlock your innermost fears.

UNDEAD PRESS

Where the Dead
Never Sleep

UNDEADPRESS.COM

THE PLACE TO GO FOR ZOMBIE AND APOCALYPTIC FICTION

  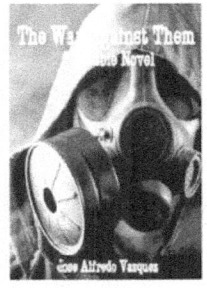

LIVING DEAD PRESS

WHERE THE DEAD WALK

www.livingdeadpress.com

ZOMBIES, MONSTERS, CREATURES OF THE NIGHT

OPEN CASKET PRESS

OPEN CASKET PRESS.COM
THE NEW NAME IN HORROR